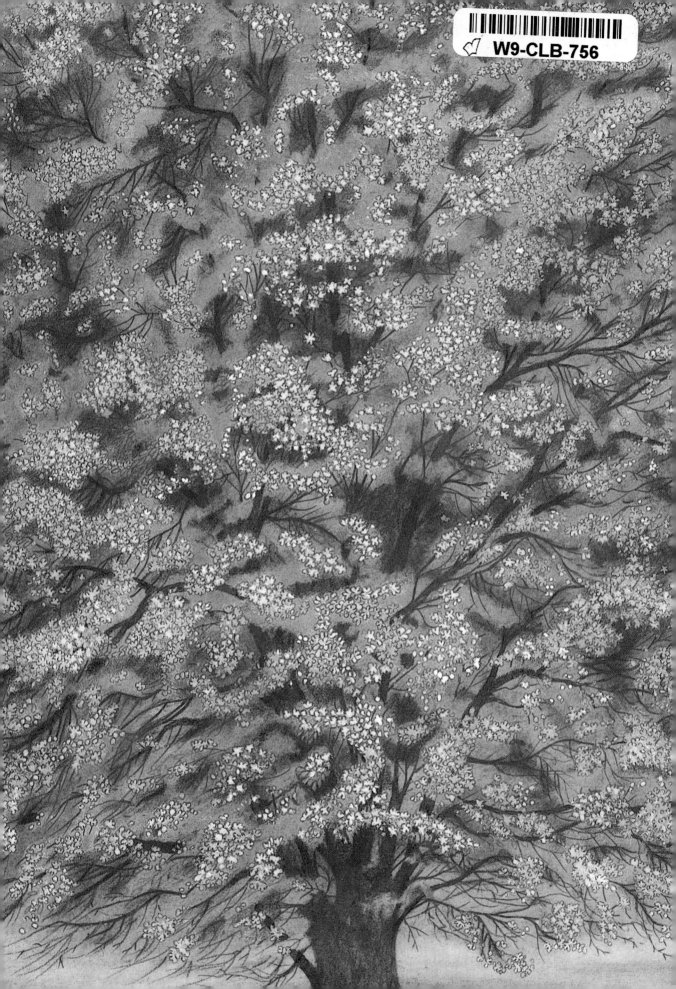

Proud Knight,
Fair Lady

VIKING KESTREL

Published by the Penguin Group
Viking Penguin Inc., 40 West 23rd Street, New York, New York 10010, U.S.A.
Penguin Books Ltd, 27 Wrights Lane, London W8 5TZ, England
Penguin Books Australia Ltd, Ringwood, Victoria, Australia
Penguin Books Canada Ltd, 2801 John Street, Markham, Ontario, Canada L3R 1B4
Penguin Books (N.Z.) Ltd, 182-190 Wairau Road, Auckland 10, New Zealand

Penguin Books Ltd, Registered Offices: Harmondsworth, Middlesex, England

First published in Great Britain by Century Hutchinson Ltd., 1989

First American edition in 1989

10 9 8 7 6 5 4 3 2 1   1 2 3 4 5 6 7 8 9 10
1 3 5 7 9 10 8 6 4 2

Translation copyright © Naomi Lewis, 1989
Illustrations copyright © Angela Barrett, 1989
All rights reserved
Library of Congress catalog card number: 88−50881
ISBN 0−670−82656−1

Printed and bound in West Germany by
Mohndruck Graphische Betriebe GMBH
Set in Caslon

PROUD KNIGHT, FAIR LADY

The Twelve Laïs of Marie de France

Translated by Naomi Lewis
Illustrated by Angela Barrett

VIKING KESTREL

CONTENTS

Introduction

No one has yet tracked down, beyond question, the identity of that tantalising character, Marie de France. We know that she was French-born, living in Norman England; we know too she wrote these lays in the later half of the twelfth century (that is, about a hundred years after the Norman Conquest) and that they were immensely popular in courtly circles on both sides of the Channel. 'Her work is loved everywhere,' wrote a contemporary, rather sourly; 'counts and barons and knights greatly admire it and hold it dear. . . . And they take such pleasure in it, that they have it read, and often copied.' It was too secular for his pious tastes. But the lays were to influence many later writers, Chaucer among them (see his *The Franklin's Tale*) and they fascinate and intrigue us still today.

Yet the author herself remains a mystery. 'My name is Marie,' she writes in the Epilogue to the lays; 'I am of France.' No more than that. Who was she? Books that attempt to answer this riddle and scholarly studies of her work fill columns in reference libraries. Still quite a few facts can be found in the tales themselves. The lays are dedicated to a king; this king would at the time be Henry II of England, who married Eleanor of Aquitaine in 1152. In Eleanor's time particularly the court was an exciting one for writers, thinkers, musicians. (Except for this, we might think that King Henry scarcely deserves Marie's tribute.) But whatever else we learn from the lays, it is clear that Marie was a very definite personality, well-read in several languages, clever, travelled, with an eager, restless mind and original views. What was the cause of her grief and sorrow? For she speaks of undertaking the task (of composing tales) as a means of warding off suffering. Sadly, we still do not know. Whether or not she leaves a clue within you must decide for yourself.

What is a lay? This is a fair enough question, since the term has long dropped out of use. Scott, to be sure, used it often (see *The Lay of the Last Minstrel*) and Macaulay wrote his *Lays of Ancient Rome* but each dealt with bygone themes. Rather confusingly, the same word is given both for Marie's own tales and for her sources. Yet there *is* a difference. The 'lay' from which she plucked an idea was a tale or song, perhaps half verse, half prose, essentially given with music, and sung by a court harpist or journeying minstrel. A lay, in Marie's sense, was a carefully constructed narrative of a particular happening. She wrote in the current Anglo-Norman French, not in Latin. All were in eight-syllabled rhyming couplets:

> *'Lady,' the bird said, 'have no fear,*
> *The hawk is noble, with no peer.*
> *His mysteries you may not read,*
> *But with him you are safe indeed.'*

Marie was basically a storyteller, not a writer of songs. Her special concern was with the theme of love, and with the lives that it entered and transformed. But her sources were not as simple as she suggests. When she speaks, as she so often does, of long ago, bygone days, ancient times, we have to recall that she herself (from our own view) belonged to a far-off, almost legendary period. Shakespeare himself would not be born for another four hundred years. The very thought of the distant past from Marie's stance can give us now a shiver of strangeness. Caught in her lays (and not only through the harpists' songs) are fragments of lost literature from well before the Conquest, of legends, ballads, epics, folklore and fairy tale. These would be mainly of Celtic origin, from Cornwall, Wales, Scotland, the wild coast of Brittany itself. All these places come into her tales. She used her own wide reading too; romances, chronicles, Arthurian lore, the Latin classics (Ovid especially), the Bible, lives of Saints. But the final product is unmistakably her own.

Though all the twelve tales are love stories, set in the courtly world that she knew well, no two are really alike. Sometimes the lady makes the first advance (though properly, through a trusted confidant) – and this seems natural enough. Marie certainly offers her own variations on the rules of chivalry, but she keeps to two absolutes: loyalty to one's liege lord; total fidelity in love. If these conflict, the second, perhaps, has the higher claim. For love has precedence over all else. Marriage, too? Yes, if the lady has been forced into loveless wedlock with an old and jealous spouse. But love has its laws and must keep within the bounds of seemliness (*mesure*). Most tragedies are based on a human flaw, and, as we see in these tales, obstinacy and vainglory (*The Two Lovers*), the failure to keep a secret (*Bisclavret*), the attempt to kill an excellent husband (*Equitan*) – such immoderacies bring disaster. Still, where love is true (as in *Lanval*, that marvellous wish-dream story) the wrong may be forgiven.

What marks her as a true storyteller, is her gift for suddenly holding and focusing light on an episode; this brings an immediate life to the tale, however strange the plot. *Lanval* abounds in such moments: the knight, perplexed, in the unknown green meadow, where his horse begins to tremble, for this is the place where human and fairy world meet; the queen and her maidens descending the stair to meet the knights below (a perfect Burne-Jones theme), and of course the final magnificent scene when the fairy arrives with superb assurance to rescue her human lover and take him to Avalon. In *Le Fresne* – another excellent tale, we remember how news of his neighbour's wife's twin births is brought to the knight's high table; we see in our minds the infant laid in the ash-tree fork, and the porter finding the bundle. And who could forget, in *Yonec*, the lady's leap of twenty feet from the tower and her following of the trail of blood into doleful and haunting regions? In *Eliduc* (among much else), the storm-tossed boat lives on, with its crew who wish to cast out the unlucky girl; so, without question, does the weasel by the tomb, that brings a magic flower to restore its mate to life. Perhaps the most moving and delicate scene is that of the lovers' meeting in the wood in *Chevrefoil* where so little and so much appears to happen. But less significant instances hold the imagination. When Milun's messenger goes through the hall with the swan (an odd sight, certainly) he passes two knights playing chess. They are so absorbed in the game that they do not notice him. A fine mediaeval detail.

Fairy tale characters tend to be stock figures, but Marie's seem often drawn from actual life. The good-natured husband in *Le Fresne* who wastes no time in reproaches but joyfully welcomes a new-found daughter is real enough; so too are the jolly knights in *Lanval* who stand bail for the knight and do their best to cheer the mournful fellow. Servants are no ciphers either (their place in fiction should never be underrated): remember the maid-companion in *Guigemar* who briskly brings the moping lovers together, and the resourceful girl in *Le Fresne*, who deals with her lady's awkward problem and takes the infant twin a long night's journey away to a distant abbey.

But with this human observation a thread of magic runs through the lays; it gives them a place in the great tradition of fairy tale. Here is a prince who comes in response to a lady's wish, but in the guise of a hawk – a powerful story. Here is a swan that for twenty years takes messages between two divided lovers. A weasel shows a human how to bring the dead to life by means of a magic flower. A white hind reproaches its hunter-killer and (very rightly as we now would think) lays a curse upon him:

> You, vassal, who have injured me,
> I now pronounce your destiny.
> Never will your torment end
> That none can ease and none can mend.
> No salve, no draught, no herb can cure
> The wound you earned and must endure.
> The shaft that slew me pierced your thigh.
> You must know grief, but I must die.

A magic ship brings lover to lover with no man at its helm. A fairy gives her chosen knight some of the classic magical gifts: the ever-full purse; the power to call the loved one by a wish. A knight at times becomes a wolf – interestingly, a *good* wolf, one of the few of its kind not miscast in myth as a villain. Even the tokens exchanged by a knight and lady take on a supernatural force of their own; no hand but the lover's can ever untie the knotted cloth.

Today, what appeals to us most in these lays of so long ago? The sieges of the heart? These greatly pleased the hearers and readers of Marie's time, and will always be a high theme of verse and story. But now we find something more. The past, if we are honest, can really be more mysterious than the future. We can guess at tomorrow (as fiction writers have been doing for years), but the mists and silences of the past are baffling. Still, grief and hope, delight and wonder are much the same for all humans, whatever the century or the place. We read these tales as marvellous fairy lore, for magic of this kind outlasts all other fashions. But we also hear a voice from eight hundred years ago, and it still rings clearly; we step into a hall, a forest, a castle of that time, and no one turns us away.

NAOMI LEWIS

GUIGEMAR

ou know that in bygone times the Bretons made lays of the happenings in their land. A good story is wasted if it is not well told. So I tell you now, in as fair words as I can, the first of these true tales from Brittany long ago.

At the time when this lay begins, Brittany, so often at war with its neighbours, was ruled by King Hoilas. His chief adviser and friend was a trusted baron, Oridial, lord of Liun. This worthy knight had two children, a son, Guigemar, and a daughter, Nöguent, a girl of rare beauty. The son himself was no less beautiful; there could not have been a more handsome young man in the kingdom. His parents loved him almost beyond reason. But the time came when, like all well-born

youths, he had to enter the service of another king. Here too he was loved by all for his charm, good sense and unfailing valour.

When Guigemar reached the right age, and was judged to have proper skills and wisdom, the king dubbed him knight, giving him whatever arms and accoutrements he desired. Then, after generously handing out gifts, Guigemar made his way to Flanders. Since there were always wars and battles in that land, it was a good place for a young knight to win renown. It was soon agreed that he had no equal in knightly prowess, no, not in Burgundy, Anjou, Lorraine or Gascony either. But one thing perplexed his friends and family. He showed not the slightest interest in matters of the heart. There could not have been a maiden in the world, however highborn and lovely, who would not joyfully have granted him her love. But he seemed to care nothing for women. Both friends and strangers shrugged; best to leave him alone. They had to agree that love was not this valiant fighter's battlefield.

At the height of his triumphs, Guigemar decided to go home, to see his father and his lord, his mother and his sister; they had longed for his return. He had been back for a month or so when he had a sudden wish to go hunting. That evening he called together his knights, his huntsmen and beaters, and in the dawn they all set off for the forest. Guigemar loved the chase. A large stag was sighted, and the hounds were unleashed. While the huntsmen went ahead, Guigemar waited in the rear, to be ready to shoot an arrow. Then, in the heart of a bush he perceived a hind and her fawn. She was completely white, with antlers like those of a stag. When she heard the dogs, she leapt out. As she did so, Guigemar shot an arrow which struck the animal's forehead. She fell to the ground, but the arrow rebounded, piercing

Guigemar in the thigh. He dismounted and lay on the grass, just beside the injured hind. Then the suffering creature spoke these words.

'Alas, I am mortally hurt. Wretched vassal, you who struck the blow, this shall be your doom. Nothing will cure the wound in your thigh, no potion, herb or root, no doctor or physician. Your only hope is to find a woman ready to endure the utmost anguish for your sake, and you in turn must suffer as much for her – so desperately that even those who know the pangs of love would tremble at your pain. Now go; get out of this wood, and leave me in peace.'

Guigemar was greatly disturbed. He did not wish to die of his injury, yet where was a cure to be found? He could not imagine a woman who might ever stir him to love, let alone make him suffer for love – nor one who would endure untold pain for his sake. He called his squire to his side. 'My friend,' he said, 'ride quickly and fetch my companions. I wish to speak to them.' As soon as the young man had gone, Guigemar bound his wound tightly with his shirt, groaning with pain as he did so. Then he mounted his horse and rode off in a new direction; he did not want to be seen, or stopped or followed. A green path ran through the wood; it led him to an open plain. He saw a cliff and a mountain; with water flowing below. An inlet formed a harbour – and there was the sail of a ship. Coming nearer, he perceived that the vessel was ready to take to sea; inside and out it was so perfectly caulked that it seemed without joints. It was a strange and beautiful vessel. The pegs and rails were of ebony, worth more than their weight in gold. The sail was all of silk; how lovely it looked unfurled!

Yet Guigemar felt uneasy. Never had he known of any port for ships in that region. He dismounted from his horse and slowly climbed aboard, still in great pain. He expected to find men in charge, but not a soul was there. Then, in the centre of the vessel he saw a bed, one that might have been designed for Solomon himself. The posts and head board were of cypress wood and white ivory, inlaid with gold. Gold threads were woven into the silken quilt. The other coverings were of rich and lustrous material of a rarity beyond price. As for the pillow – well, no one who had placed his head upon it would ever have white hair. Over all was a cover of sable, lined with Alexandrinian silk. On the ship's prow were two candelabra with lighted candles; they were wrought in purest gold. A fortune could not have bought even the smaller of the two.

Guigemar looked and marvelled. Then, because his pain was great, he lay down on the bed for a while to rest. Presently he rose, intending to leave the ship – but he could not; it was on the high seas, with a fair wind speeding it on.

What could he do? His heart sank. There was no chance of returning to land. His wound tormented him more and more, but he had to accept his fate. He prayed to God to protect him, then he lay down again and slept. Though he did not know it yet, by nightfall he would reach the place where his cure would begin.

The ship stopped, of its own accord, at the foot of an ancient city, capital of the realm. The lord who ruled over it was a very old man. His wife was of noble birth, courtly, wise and beautiful, and her husband was devoured by jealousy, in the manner of old men with young wives. He went to lengths beyond all reason to keep her from the world. In a garden that bordered the dungeon keep was a small enclosure, surrounded on all sides by a thick high wall of green marble. The one small opening in the wall was guarded day and night. On the further side lay the sea, which prevented any chance of entering or leaving, except by boat. Inside the enclosure the old man had designed a room both beautiful and strange, with a chapel leading into it. The walls of the room were covered in paintings in which Venus, goddess of love, was shown pointing out the duties and obligations of young wives. One painting portrayed the goddess angrily throwing a book into blazing flames, because it gave different advice from her own.

In this room the lady was kept imprisoned. She had only one attendant, her husband's niece, a lively, intelligent maiden. The two girls were close friends. No one else could enter or leave; no one could escape from the walled prison. An aged priest guarded the key to the door; he also recited prayers and served at table. Now it happened that, one afternoon, the lady wandered into the narrow garden with her maid; they gazed down at the sea, and saw a strange ship rising and falling on the waves as it reached the harbour. No one seemed to be steering. The lady was afraid; her colour came and went and she wished to turn and run. But her companion was much bolder. 'Be calm,' she said. 'There is nothing to fear.'

They crept out on to the wave-washed shore, and the maiden took off her cloak and climbed aboard the vessel. She searched about, but found only one human creature – a sleeping knight, so pale and still that at first she thought him dead.

She returned to the lady and told her what she had seen. The lady answered, 'Let us go to the ship together. If the knight is dead, he must be given burial. But if he is alive, he will speak and explain the mystery.' They boarded the ship and stood before the bed. The lady gazed down sadly; she grieved at the death of one so handsome and so young. But was he really dead? She placed her hand on his heart and felt it beat; the body was warm, not cold. Her touch awoke the knight and he greeted her courteously.

The lady, always in fear of her husband, was anxious and trembling, but she spoke to the stranger graciously, and asked how he came to be in that crewless ship. 'What land are you from? Has war made you an exile?'

'Lady,' said Guigemar, 'I am no exile or outlaw. If you want me to tell my story, I shall do so. I come from Brittany. Early this morning, I went hunting and shot a white hind. The arrow rebounded and pierced me in the thigh, so deeply that I fear I shall never recover. The hind lamented the mortal hurt I had dealt it and put a curse upon me: that my wound will never heal, except through the love of an unknown damsel, and the suffering both of the damsel and myself. I do not know who the damsel is nor where she may be found. But when I heard the words of doom, I hastened out of the wood; I saw this ship in a harbour, and foolishly went on board. It sailed away with no other human soul. No one steered. No one was there to steer. Now I must have reached land, but I do not know where I am, or where to go. Fair lady, in God's name tell me what you can.'

'Sir knight,' the lady said, 'I would gladly help you if I could. This city belongs to my husband, so does all the surrounding country. He is a man of high lineage, but very old, and jealous beyond all reason. That is why I am imprisoned here, with no chance of escape. There is only one door, and an old priest keeps the key. All that I have is a bedroom and a chapel and, for company, this damsel, my loyal friend. But if you wish to remain until you are ready to travel, and can keep well hidden, we will give you shelter and whatever help we can.'

When Guigemar heard these words he thanked the lady gratefully. He raised himself from the bed, and the two damsels helped him to walk, though with some difficulty. They took him to the bedroom and placed him on the maiden's couch, which lay behind a curtain in that room. They brought water in golden basins, washed the wound, then bound it tightly with fine white linen. When the evening meal was brought in, the maiden put aside sufficient for the knight.

So now he had food and drink and treatment for his wound. But he could not rest. Another weapon had pierced him, this time to the heart, the arrow of love, and the lady herself was the cause. His homeland was forgotten, so was the pain in his thigh, yet anguish made him toss and turn. His mind whirled with troubled thoughts. He could not understand why, but he knew that without the help of the lady and none other, he had no hope of a cure. 'Woe is

me!' he said. 'What shall I do? Shall I beg her to have pity on a wretched being? If she refuses, if she is haughty and proud, then I am lost indeed.' He had never known before the terrible pain of love.

The lady felt no happier than the knight. When morning came she lamented that she had not slept at all. The maiden saw at once that love was her complaint and that the stranger was the cause. The lady did not know that the knight burned with the same fever.

The girl went to the invalid's bedside. At once, he asked, 'My friend, where has your lady gone? Why is she up so early?' Then he sighed and was silent.

The maiden said, 'My lord, you are in love, that is your trouble. Do not conceal the fact too long, for you may be very near to what you seek. You love my lady. She is not unmoved by you. You are handsome. She is beautiful. But you must love her truly and constantly and, if you both keep faith with each other, this will be a proper affair of the heart.'

Guigemar replied, 'Sweet friend, help me; tell me what I am to do.' The maiden spoke cheering words, and assured him that she would do whatever she could. After mass in the chapel, the lady returned to her room and asked how the knight was faring. Was he yet awake? Her heart beat with longing.

'He has just woken,' the girl said. 'Go and visit him.' Left to themselves, she thought, they would have the chance to make their feelings known. And so it came about.

Guigemar spoke first. 'Lady,' he said, 'I am dying for love of you. If you are not willing to cure me, my death will follow.'

She answered fittingly, 'Friend, I am not accustomed to such requests. Is it right to be hasty in these matters?'

'Lady,' he said, 'the long game of courtship is for lighter love than ours.' Then he set out his case so fairly and with such reasoning that she saw good sense in his words. When he said at last, 'Let us end this debate,' the lady was of the same mind. They kissed and were friends.

Guigemar stayed with the lady for a year and a half. But fortune is faithful only to herself. One summer morning the lady said to the knight, 'Sweet friend, there are signs that we have been discovered. You must escape. But I feel a dread that once away you will find another love, while I am left here to die of grief.'

'Have no fear,' said he. 'That can never happen.'

'Then let us each give the other a pledge,' said she. 'I shall tie a knot in your shirt; if any woman can undo it, you have my leave to love her, whoever she may be.' He in turn gave her a belt to wear about her waist. If any man could unfasten it, that man alone had a right to be her lover.

But time was running out. A cunning chamberlain had spied through a window and had reported what he had seen. The husband was aghast. Taking three trusted men he went to his wife's room and had them break down the door. There, within, was the knight. 'Kill the fellow!' ordered the furious lord. But Guigemar seized a stout wooden pole that was used for hanging clothes and prepared to defend himself; he would have done mortal damage to all or any of them. The lord paused, looked closely at the knight, and asked how he had come to be in this secret place.

Guigemar told his story. The lord looked scornful. 'Do you really expect me to believe that nonsense? Well, if you can show me the vessel, if I can see for myself that it exists, you'll be put aboard and out you go to sea. If you perish – good! I hope you do.'

They went down to the harbour and there was the ship! Guigemar was pushed aboard and, at once, the vessel sped off again, this time making for Guigemar's own country. He disembarked and looked around. A young man who had been in his service was riding one horse and leading another. The youth dismounted and offered the other horse to the knight; they rode on together. And so Guigemar returned to his home and was greeted joyfully.

But he remained sad and downcast. His friends thought that he should marry, and tried to find a maiden who would please him, yet all this was wasted time. If a woman could undo the lady's knot – well, that was another matter. But no one could, though many hopeful damsels came to try. And the lady, what of her? The old lord now imprisoned her in a tower of dark marble, and there she spent two years in grief and solitude. 'Oh, Guigemar,' she would cry. 'It was a sad day for me when I met you. If I can ever escape, I shall drown myself in the sea that swallowed you.' For she thought that he had drowned.

One day, wild with despair, she tried the door – it was neither locked nor bolted. She went out; no one saw her go. In the harbour was the ship, and she stepped aboard. Swiftly she was carried along, until the vessel reached a port in Brittainy. Just above was a fine strong castle. The lord of the castle, Meriaduc by name, was waging war against a neighbour; he had risen at dawn to direct the day's battle and, looking down, saw the ship. He sent for his chamberlain, and with him climbed a ladder and went aboard. Within, all alone, was a lady, lovely as a fairy. He led her to his castle, delighted by his discovery. She was so beautiful! She was also of noble birth, that was clear,

whatever the reason for her strange situation. He treated her with honour and courtesy, gave her beautiful clothes, every attention. His own young sister, a lively and charming girl, was made her attendant. But when he spoke of love she would not hear his pleas.

At last she told him of the pledge and showed him the belt; saying that only the man who could unfasten the buckle would be her lover. Meriaduc promptly tried and failed; he was vexed. 'There is another such character in this land,' he said, 'a knight of great renown who refuses to take a wife unless the woman can undo a knot in his clothing. I suspect it was you who tied that knot.'

When the lady heard these words, she felt faint with joy. Guigemar was alive!

Now that the test was known, many knights came to undo the belt but not one could succeed. Meriaduc was curious to know the truth. He proclaimed a tournament, and asked the valiant Guigemar if he would come to assist him against his enemies. Guigemar agreed, and he arrived with a retinue of more than a hundred knights. Meriaduc lodged him in his tower, with every honour, then arranged for his sister to come to the hall, and bring the lady with her. The two arrived hand in hand. The lady looked sad and pale, but when Guigemar saw her he stood still, saying to himself, 'Is this my sweet friend, my heart, my life, my lost and beautiful lady, whom I loved, and who loved me? But no, it cannot be. What could have brought her here? I am living in a dream as always. Yet I have a great desire to speak with her.'

He went forward and begged her to sit down beside him. Meriaduc laughed and called out, 'Why not let the lady see if she can untie that knot?' Guigemar ordered the garment to be brought. The lady saw it; she knew it well, but in that assembly she had not courage to try. Meriaduc called out, 'Come, lady, see what you can do.' She put her hand on the knot, and at once it was untied.

Guigemar was amazed, but still could not believe that what he so much wanted had come about. 'Beloved,' he said, 'I hope that I do not dream, that it really is yourself by my side. Have you still the belt which I fastened with my own hands? She had, and it came apart at his touch. She told him of all the misfortune that she had undergone since his escape, and how she had reached this place in the magic ship.

Guigemar rose. 'My lords,' he said, 'I have found at last a friend whom I thought I had lost for ever. I beg you Meriaduc, to restore her to me. I will gladly become your vassal and serve you, for two or three years, with a hundred knights or more.'

Meriaduc said, 'I am not in such straits that I need this kind of bargain. I found the lady and I shall keep her.'

When Guigemar heard this he departed with all his knights, leaving a challenge to Meriaduc. He gathered not only his own men, but Meriaduc's opponents who had come to fight in the tournament. They attacked and captured the castle and the whole of the town was won over. Guigemar was now free to ride away with his love. The curse had expired and joy awaited them both.

The lay of Guigemar was composed from this remarkable tale. It is performed on harp and rote* and the melody is pleasing to the ear.

---

*A five-stringed harp, not unlike a zither.

Le Fresne

shall tell you now about Le Fresne, a very curious tale. You may have heard the lay. Who was Le Fresne? Be patient; you shall hear.

In bygone times, in Brittany, there lived two knights, both from the same region. They were neighbours, for their lands adjoined; they were also friends. Both had wealth and power; both were noble and valiant. Now it happened that the wife of one of these worthy knights conceived, and in due time gave birth to twins, both boys. The father was overjoyed, and straight away sent a message to his neighbour inviting him to be godfather to one of them; moreover, if the knight was willing, the child would be named after him.

When the messenger arrived, the neighbour knight and his household were in the hall, at dinner. The page knelt down before the high table and told what he had come to tell. The knight was in high good spirits at the news. 'Thanks be to God!' he said, and he gave orders for the messenger to be rewarded with the gift of a fine horse. But the knight's wife, who sat beside him, had other thoughts. She was a proud, quick-tempered woman, easily stung to rage and jealousy. Now, she gave a scornful laugh and before the entire household, she uttered words that she would long regret. 'So help me God,' she said, 'I am amazed that our worthy neighbour has not been more discreet about the shameful business. How could he let it be known that his wife had so dishonoured him and disgraced herself! Two infants born at a single birth! Everyone knows that no woman has ever had, nor ever will have such a misfortune unless she has loved two men.'

Her husband stared at her as if thunderstruck. Then he spoke sharply. 'Lady,' he said, 'stop this wild talk. You must not speak this way. You are slandering a lady of excellent reputation – and that is the truth of the matter.' But, since everyone had fallen silent while the two were speaking, the whole of the household heard the calumny.

Soon it was whispered about the town, and then beyond, until it was common talk all over Brittany. All this did the foolish wife no good; every woman, rich or poor, high or low, reviled and hated her. You can hardly be surprised! And, as I said, she was soon to have a further reason for wishing she had been silent. Wait, and you shall learn.

Meanwhile the messenger returned, and gave his lord a full account of the happening. The knight was troubled; he too began to have doubts about his unfortunate lady, and to treat her with an unkindness that she did not deserve. You see what harm can come from false and spiteful words.

But listen to this! In that same year, the evil-speaking wife herself conceived, and in nine months' time gave birth not to one child, but two, both of them girls. She was distraught. 'Unhappy woman that I am!' she cried. 'What shall I do? If this is known, I shall be a laughing stock, disgraced through all the land. My husband and his people will never believe that I am innocent – and this is my own fault entirely. When I accused all women, I accused myself. Did I not say that when two children are born at a single birth, the mother must have loved two men? And here am I now in that plight. Oh, the folly of uttering lies and slander! They carry their own punishment. I harmed a woman more honourable than myself.

'Oh, oh, what can I do? I shall have to destroy one of the children. It will be easier to make my own peace with God than to endure disgrace and shame and mockery.' So she went on.

Her women tried to calm and comfort her – 'Lady,' they said, 'you cannot do such a deed. To kill your child is no light matter. Wait a while. Time will bring other answers.'

Among her attendants was a maid to whom the lady felt very close. The girl was of excellent family; she had been with her mistress many years and loved her well; indeed, she was her kindest helper and most faithful friend. The lady's happiness was her own, so were the lady's sorrows. So when she heard the lamenting and crying she thought for a while, then offered some practical counsel. 'Lady,' she said, 'you must stop tormenting yourself. I shall take one of the children far away, and you need have no more fear of shame. The child will not be harmed, I promise you. I will leave her in a church; some good man will find her, and please God, give her a home.'

The lady was overjoyed at these words. 'You are the best of friends,' she said. 'I shall reward you well.'

Since they wished it to be known that the child was of noble birth, they wrapped it first in a cloth of finest linen; over that they wound a length of matchless silk, flower-embroidered, soft and lustrous. The husband had brought it back from Constantinople. Then, with a silken ribbon, the lady tied to the infant's arm a great ring made from an ounce of pure gold, set with an amethyst. An inscription was engraved within; certainly, whoever found the child would know that it was highborn. Nothing more could be done, and the damsel took the infant to her own place.

That night, when all was dark and the household slept, she stole out with the sleeping child, made her way beyond the town and took a certain path which led right through the forest. By keeping carefully to this road she emerged at last on the distant side, a place unknown to her. Far off to the right she heard the barking of dogs, then the crowing of cocks; here, she knew, must be a village or a town. As fast as she could – for it was nearly dawn – she went in the direction of the noise. Presently she saw that she was approaching a fair and noble city. She entered, and came to a great abbey, with every sign of wealth and rich endowment. It housed (though she did not know it) a community of nuns with an Abbess over them. The damsel gazed about her at the mighty walls and towers, at the church with its belfry, then she knelt at the church door and began to pray. 'Lord God,' she said, 'may it be your will that this child is kept from harm.'

Then, the door being closed, she looked about her and saw an ash tree, thick leaved, wide spreading; it had been planted to give good shade and this it did. The trunk, she noticed, branched out into four – ah, there was the answer. She gathered up the child in its wrappings, ran to the tree, and placed it carefully in this natural cradle. Once more she commended it to heavenly care, then set out on the long journey back to make report to her lady. There for a while we must leave them, and return to the infant child.

There was a porter at the abbey who had the task of opening the door of the church for those who came to service. That day, he rose very early, lit the lamps and candles, rang the bell and opened the great door. Something caught his eye in the ash tree – a bundle of clothes perhaps; a thief might have hidden them up there. He made his way to the tree as fast as his stiff legs would take him, and put out his hand. Ah – it was no roll of stuff but a warm living infant! 'God be thanked!' he cried. Then he drew forth the child and carried it back to his home.

He had a daughter, recently widowed, with an infant of her own. He called to her, 'Rise, daughter! Blow up the fire; light candles. I have just found a little child in the ash-tree fork. Look, here it is! Keep it warm, give it some milk, bathe it in warm water.' The daughter was up at once, made

the fire ablaze, then fed and tended the child. As she was washing it she found the gold ring tied to its arm. They looked at the ring, and at the fine embroidered cloth; it was a child of noble birth, no doubt about that.

Later that day, after the service, the porter waited for the Abbess to leave the church. As soon as he could catch her attention he told her of his strange find in the tree. 'Bring me the child,' she ordered, 'with all its clothing, just as you found it.' The porter did as she asked. The Abbess looked at the infant carefully, then at last she spoke. 'This child will be brought up here, as my niece. But the secret must be kept. You must forget what you have seen.'

So the little girl grew up within the abbey as the niece of the Abbess. She was known as Le Fresne, which means ash tree. And when she left childhood behind her, there was no lovelier maiden in Brittany, nor one more courtly in grace and manner. No one of noblest birth could have been better taught, or more accomplished in all that she did. This gentle and modest girl was admired and loved by all who encountered her, and who can wonder?

Now at Dol in Upper Brittany there lived a certain lord, best of men and masters; you would not find one better liked anywhere. You want to know his name? I shall tell you. In his own region he was known as Gurun. He had heard so much praise of the convent maiden that he began to love even the thought of her. One day, as he returned from a tournament, he passed the abbey and had the idea of asking to see the girl of whom everyone spoke well. The Abbess, knowing the lord, permitted this. But nothing had prepared him for the sight of the girl herself. How beautiful she was! How courteous was her manner – how distinguished! He burned to win her love. If he failed, his life would not be worth living. Yet what could he do? If he kept returning, the Abbess would be suspicious and he would never be able to see her again.

An idea came to him. He would donate much wealth and many acres of land to the abbey, gifts of lasting value, giving him an overlord's rights to a dwelling in the walls; he also bought a personal place in the community. Do not be mistaken – it was not to obtain remission of his sins. No, he had other motives.

So now he was able to see the maiden often, and to talk with her: but such talk, such begging and pleading, such allurements and promises! It is no marvel that this charming man, benefactor and overlord, soon gained what he most desired. When he knew that he was certain of her love, he said to her one day, 'Sweet one, you have given me your heart, and more. Now come and make your home with me. If your aunt the Abbess learns of our meetings she will be grieved and offended. Take the advice of one who loves you, and come with me to my house. Have no fear. I shall never fail you. Whatever you want shall be yours.'

The young girl loved him deeply and agreed to go; together, they left the abbey, and journeyed to his castle. But she did not forget to bring two things, the embroidered silken cloth and the gold ring. The Abbess had given them to her, telling her how, as an infant, she had been placed by unknown hands in the ash-tree boughs, with only these two possessions, and how she, the Abbess, had brought her up as her niece. The girl had taken cloth and ring and put them carefully into a casket; now they came with her.

The days and months passed joyfully at the castle, for the lord Gurun loved his damsel dearly and cherished her tenderly. Indeed, she was loved and honoured by everyone in the household, high and low, for her goodness and her charm. But outside there were some murmurings. A time came when certain of his landed knights came to Gurun saying that he should take a wife of noble birth and free himself from the entanglement. He should have a legal heir to inherit his lands; indeed, if he did not do as they wished they would no longer consider him their lord, nor do him service.

At last he agreed to do their will. And so they looked about to find a fitting damsel. Soon they returned. 'Lord,' they said, 'not far from this place lives a worthy man, equal in birth and substance to yourself. He has one daughter, his only child and heir; much land will come to her. The maiden is known as La Coudre, the hazel tree. There is no more beautiful girl in all the land. You really should give up the ash tree and take the hazel instead. Now, say the word of approval and we shall speak for the damsel on your behalf. Please God, we shall very soon bring her back to be your wife.' So they approached the maiden's father and made negotiations for the marriage.

Ah me! They meant well, these worthy knights; but it was a thousand pities that they did not know the history of the two young girls. They were none other than the twin sisters separated so soon after birth. I must say that La Coudre knew nothing of Le Fresne as she prepared for the wedding. And Fresne herself? When she learnt of her lord's approaching marriage she made no comment, and behaved with her usual quiet courtesy. But the whole of the household, not only her own attendants but knights, squires, pages and serving boys were grieved and angered to think that they might be losing her.

The wedding day arrived. Many guests had been summoned, among them the Archbishop of Dol, who was Gurun's vassal. The bride came with her mother, but that lady was uneasy. She knew of the girl Fresne and of Gurun's love for her and she feared that she might try to make a rift between Gurun and her daughter after the marriage. Fresne, she decided, must be made to leave the house as soon as possible; Gurun could marry her off to some suitable man quite easily. Anyhow, by whatever means, the place must be rid of her.

After the wedding ceremony there were feastings and merrymakings. People looked at Fresne; but she was so calm and gracious, so ready to help, that they could only marvel. Indeed, when the bride's mother saw the damsel for herself, her heart was strangely moved. She felt respect, admiration, even love, though she could not have said why. 'If I had known the quality of this young girl,' she told herself, 'I would not have feared for my daughter. What's more, I would not have agreed to the marriage if it took her from her lord.'

Towards evening, attendants went to prepare the marriage bed, and Fresne came to see that this was properly done. She perceived that they were placing over the top a piece of coarse material of a kind used for making clothes. Surely something better than this could be found! She opened the coffer which held her treasures, took out and unfolded the rare embroidered silk and laid it over the bed where her lord and the bride would lie. Then

the Archbishop came to bless the bed, for this was part of his duty.

When all had gone from the room the lady brought her daughter to prepare her for the night. She saw the silken covering and stood still. Only one such piece was known to her – the one which had wrapped the infant she had lost. She called for the chamberlain. 'Tell me the truth,' she said. 'Where did this coverlet come from?'

'Lady,' he said, 'the damsel Fresne took it from a coffer and placed it here. She did not like the cover we had used. I think the cloth is hers.'

'Find the damsel Fresne,' she said, 'and bring her to me.'

The girl came and the lady demanded of her, 'Fair damsel, I want you to tell me truly. This silken coverlet – where was it found? How did you come to possess it? Did someone give it to you? If someone gave it, who was the giver?'

The girl said, 'Lady, it was given to me by my aunt the Abbess; she told me to keep it carefully. Those who sent me into care gave me that silken cloth and a ring.'

'Fair damsel,' said the other, 'may I see the ring?'

'Gladly,' said the girl. She took it from the coffer and the lady gazed at it silently, holding it in her hand. She knew the ring and the silken cloth all too well.

But at last she spoke, saying, for all to hear, 'Fair damsel, you are my daughter.' Then she fell back in a swoon.

When she recovered she sent for her husband; he hastened to her, very alarmed. As soon as he entered the room, she knelt before him and clasped his feet. 'Husband,' she said, 'I beg you to forgive me for my sin.' The knight was puzzled; he could not imagine what she meant.

'Lady,' he said, 'what is all this? There has never been anything but good between us. If you want something pardoned, so be it. Only tell me what you wish.' He was an easy-going man.

'Husband, lord,' she said, 'now that I have your forgiveness I will tell my story. Listen carefully. Once, out of hate and spite, I did my neighbour a wrong. I slandered her for giving birth to twin children, but the injury turned on me. This is the truth that I have so long kept hidden. When I in turn came to give birth, I also had not one but two, both daughters. I dared not let this be known! So I had one infant taken away; she was left in a church with two possessions: the embroidered cloth that you brought from the East, and the ring you gave me when you first spoke with me. But now the secret must come out. Listen! I have found the cloth and the ring, and with them my daughter, lost by my own folly. She is here before you, the damsel Fresne, so noble, wise and fair – the real love of the knight to whom we betrothed our other daughter.'

The husband said, 'This is good news! We must all rejoice. Never has anything made me so happy as this finding of our lost girl. What's more, God has granted us a second gift; he has saved us from adding a second wrong to the first. Daughter, come here!'

So Fresne at last learned the truth about her birth. When the mystery of her story was revealed she felt radiant with wonder and delight. As for her father, he could not wait to share the joyful news, and to mend what needed mending. First he went to the lord Gurun to tell him the whole strange tale; with him he took the Archbishop.

The knight was overcome with happiness at the news about his beloved Fresne. 'Let us do nothing tonight,' said the Archbishop. 'Tomorrow I will unjoin the pair who were married this morning.' All agreed, and the next day this was done. The lord Gurun then took as wife his true love Fresne, and the knight her father gave her away at the wedding. He made over to her a full half of his inheritance. Her mother too was at the celebration, so was her new-found sister. Presently they returned to their own place, and a worthy husband, rich and noble, was found for La Coudre, the hazel tree.

When all this came to be known it was made into the lay called 'Le Fresne', You may have heard it sung; now you know the truth of the tale itself.

BISCLAVRET

ow, a tale that must especially have a place in these lays is the one called 'Bisclavret'. Well, that is the Breton name; the Normans call it 'Garwaf'; the English would say 'Werewolf'. In bygone days you could hear many a tale about men who changed into wolves and made their home in the woods. It is not only in legends that we hear of them, but in real histories too; this is such a one. Oh, it is a strange creature, the man-wolf. Beware of enraging it, for then it could destroy you. At other times, though. . . . But no more delay: I want to tell you the story.

In Brittany, in bygone days, there lived a certain baron, admired and praised by all who knew him. He was, it seems, both good and handsome; in every way he behaved as befits a noble knight. The lord of his region made him a close friend and adviser; his neighbours loved him well. His wife was well born and beautiful, a worthy partner for him, you would say, and they loved each other well. Yet there was one mystery about the man, and it troubled the lady greatly. For three days in each week he disappeared. Where did he go? What did he do? Neither she, nor anyone in the household, friend or servant, had any clue to the answer.

One day, when he had returned from his weekly absence, and greeted her joyfully, she took courage to question him. 'Dear husband,' she said, 'my lord and love, I long to ask you something, yet I dare not, so much do I fear to anger you.'

When he heard these words, he drew her towards him and kissed her. 'Sweet lady,' he said, 'ask what you will. If I know the answer, you shall have it.'

'Ah,' said she, 'you lift a load from my heart. My lord, on those days when you are away I am so weighed down with grief, I have such fear that I shall never see you again, that I shall soon die of this torment. Tell me, I beg you, where do you go? What lures you from me? Do you go to meet a lover? If so, you wrong me and cause me sorrow.'

'Lady,' the husband said, 'for God's sake leave this matter alone. The reason for my going is none that you could imagine. If I tell you, it will put me in great danger. I shall lose your love; I may lose life itself.' When the lady heard these words she was aghast, and was all the more determined to learn the secret. Again and again, using all her wiles, she begged, she coaxed, she wheedled, until at last he could hold out no longer, and began to tell his story.

'My tale is a strange one,' he said. 'On the days when I leave you, I become a wolf. I enter the great forest and there, in the thickest depths, away from men, I make my dwelling. I feed on roots and on such forest creatures as I can catch. Now you know the truth.'

At first the lady was silent, then she said, 'Tell me, do you go into the forest naked or clothed?'

'Lady, I go without human clothing.'

'Then tell me, in God's name, where do you leave your clothes?'

'Lady, I dare not tell you that. If I were to lose them, I would remain a wolf for ever. Unless they were returned to me, nothing could change my doom. This is why I cannot part with this secret.'

'My lord,' said she, 'you know that I love you more than the whole world. What have I done to make you lose your trust? Tell me, and share the burden of your trouble.' So persistent was she, so much did she harass him, that at last she had her way.

'Lady,' he said, 'on the edge of the wood, not far from the path that leads within, there stands an ancient chapel. It has been of great help to me. For just outside under a bush, is a wide stone slab, hollowed out in the centre. It is in that hollow, beneath the bush, that I leave my human clothes, and gather them on my return.'

When the lady heard this extraordinary story, her face burned with dread. She began to set her mind on how she could escape, for she had no wish to be wife to a man who was half a wolf. Soon, a thought came to her. There was, in that region, a certain knight who had loved her for many a day, and had shown his devotion in many ways. She had never returned his love, nor given him any sign of doing so. But now she sent a messenger bidding him to come to her.

'Friend,' she said, 'I have sweet news for you. What you have sought for so long, I now grant you. In return for your love I give you mine.'

The knight thanked her joyfully; he gave an oath of allegiance, and the two exchanged pledges. Then she revealed to him all that her husband had told her, down to the final secret, that, without his human clothing he would not return to human shape. Then she described the chapel,

bush and stone, so that the knight might take the clothing from its hiding place.

This is how Bisclavret came to be betrayed by his wife.

Where was he? He seemed to have vanished utterly, yet because he was so often absent it was generally thought that he had gone on a long journey. A few enquiries were made, but they led nowhere. Very likely he was lost in distant wars or travel. So he dropped from people's minds. And the lady married her devoted knight.

A whole year passed without undue event. Then a day came when the king went hunting, and the chase drew him into that part of the forest where Bisclavret made his home. As soon as the hounds were unleashed they scented the wolf and both hounds and hunters pursued him through the day. They were just about to capture him and would surely have torn him to pieces when he perceived the king. At once he ran towards his one-time lord and friend, and then begged for mercy. He took the stirrup in his paw and kissed the monarch's foot and leg, as if paying homage. The king was filled with awe; he called his companions to him. 'Lords,' he said, 'look at this marvel. See how courteously this wild thing behaves, and how gently it humbles itself before me. It has the mind and manners of a knight, even as it pleads for mercy. Keep back the hounds; see that no one attacks the wolf. This creature thinks; it has understanding. I place it under my protection. Make ready to go – we hunt no more today.'

Thereupon the king set out for home and Bisclavret followed, always keeping close to his royal master, and they entered the castle together. The king was delighted at the happening. His wolf was a wonder, a marvel; he loved it dearly, and charged all around to guard it well and see that it came to no harm. No one might strike it; whatever food and drink it desired must be given. As for his knights and attendants, they willingly did as he wished. Each day the wolf would settle and sleep among them – always near to the king. It was a favourite with all; what ill behaviour could ever come from so noble and gentle a creature? Wherever the king chose to go, the wolf went also; it would not be left behind. It was clear to all how much it loved its royal master.

Now comes a strange turn to the story. The king held court; all of his barons and those who held fiefs from him were summoned to show their loyalty and to take their part in the festival. Among them, splendidly dressed, was the knight who had married the wife of Bisclavret. He had no idea at all that Bisclavret himself was at the court. As soon as this knight arrived at the palace the wolf leapt towards him, seized him with his teeth and dragged him down and towards him. The knight would have been in serious trouble if the king had not called to Bisclavret to stop, and threatened him with a stick. In spite of this Bisclavret made two more attempts that day to attack the knight. All who saw were amazed; never before had the wolf behaved so discourteously to a human. 'The wolf must have good reason for his anger,' said one to another. It was generally felt that some wrong had been done to the beast, though what they did not know. However, Bisclavret gave no more trouble for the rest of the festival. Then the barons took their leave. One of the first to go, they say, was the knight. Can you wonder that Bisclavret hated him!

Not long after, the king and his wolf companion went on an expedition into the forest where Bisclavret had been found. When night fell, they stayed in a house in that region. News that the king was at hand soon reached the neighbourhood, and one who heard was the faithless wife of Bisclavret. The next morning she put on her finest clothes, took rich presents, and went to seek an audience with the king. You may imagine the scene when Bisclavret saw her! No one could have held him back. He leapt up in a frenzy, sped towards her – and hear what revenge he took! He tore the nose from her face!

Now he was threatened on all sides, and might have been destroyed if a wise man had not said to the king, 'Sire, listen to me. This beast has lived long at court, never far from your side. All of us in your household have been with him daily, except for this lady here. By the faith I owe to you, he must have some anger against the lady and her husband. She is – you must know – the wife of the knight who was so dear to you, the one who disappeared without trace. What became of him none can tell except, perhaps, the lady. Ask her why the wolf behaved as he did. Does this seem to you outside nature? Many strange things have happened in Brittany.'

The king took his advice. He held the knight in keeping, then had the lady questioned. Under duress she revealed the truth. She told her husband's story, how at times he became a wolf, how she had taken his human clothes, and so betrayed his trust. She was sure in her heart that the wolf was Bisclavret.

'Where are the missing clothes?' asked the king. 'Have you kept them safely?' The lady bowed her head. 'Then bring them now,' said the king, and this she had to do, whether she would or no. The clothes were placed before the wolf, but he took no notice.

The wise man spoke again. 'Sire,' he said, 'how can you expect this creature to change from his animal form in open view? Would you, in his place? Take him into your own apartment, have the clothes brought to him there, and leave him for a while. Then we shall see whether or not he returns to human shape.'

The king himself led Bisclavret to the royal bedroom, he left the wolf inside with the clothing, and locked the door. After sufficient time, he returned with his wise adviser and two of his nobles. What would they find? He turned the key and they entered.

There, asleep, on the royal bed, was the long-vanished knight. The king ran to embrace him, and kissed him again and again. As soon as he could, he had Bisclavret's lands restored to him — indeed, he was given more than he owned before. As for the unfortunate woman, she was ordered away from that region. The knight went with her. They had, in time, quite a number of children. They were easily recognizable, for their female children — I am not deceiving you — were born and lived without noses. Every word of the strange tale of Bisclavret is true; so long as this lay is read and heard, it will not be forgotten.

LANVAL

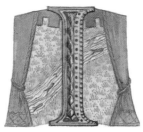

tell this tale exactly as it happened; it is well worth hearing, I promise you! It is about a young man, nobly born and noble in nature: Lanval was his name. Now it chanced that Arthur, most valiant of kings, had taken his court to Carlisle because of the Picts and Scots who were ravaging the country. Those Picts! They were forever crossing the border into England, leaving a trail of havoc and ruin. During his stay, to celebrate Pentecost, Arthur presented handsome gifts to his counts and barons and to his knights of the Round Table, that peerless company, like none other in the world. To all who had served him well he was most generous, giving them wives and lands – to all, that is, but one, and that one was Lanval. Strangely, he was forgotten, and no one reminded the king on his behalf. The reason? I can tell you in a word: envy. The knight's beauty, valour and generous nature roused the hatred of all too many at court. Some, it is true, made a show of friendship – after all, it was hard not to admire the knight – but when his luck began to turn, no one could say they were sorry.

This Lanval, I must tell you, was the son of a king, no less; but his father's court was far away. What's more, the young man had spent all his wealth in Arthur's service and was in desperate need. The king had given him nothing and he had asked for nothing. Even so, he still served Arthur loyally. But his lot was hard. Lonely, shunned, with empty purse – no wonder he was cast down. Remember that he was a stranger, far from his own land, not knowing where to turn for help and counsel.

One day, he decided to mount his horse and ride beyond the city for peace and quiet, away from the jangling court. Deep in thought, he presently found himself in a green place quite unknown to him. Through the grass ran a sparkling stream, and there he stopped. Not a soul was in sight. But the horse began to tremble violently. Why was this? The knight dismounted, loosened the saddle-girth and watched his horse roll on its back in the grass. Then he folded his cloak, put it as a pillow under his head, and lay there thinking of his troubles. Nothing could bring him comfort. Suddenly, he felt that he was not alone; lifting his head, he saw two damsels of startling beauty, gliding along the river bank towards him. He had never seen fairer ladies anywhere. They were richly dressed in close-fitting robes of a violet colour. The elder of the two carried a golden bowl, delicately made by some master craftsman, the other a fine linen cloth. They went straight to where the knight was resting and, at once, in mannerly fashion, he leapt to his feet. After some words of courtesy, they explained why they had come. 'Lanval,' said one, 'we bring you a message. Our mistress, who is as wise and noble as she is fair to look upon, has sent us here to fetch you. Look, there is her tent; we will lead you there safely.'

So the knight went with them, leaving his horse to graze as it pleased in the meadow. Soon they reached the tent – but how can I describe something so marvellous in mere words? I can only say that neither the Queen Semiramis, with all her wealth and power, nor the Emperor Octavius, could have afforded even a single one of its panels. On the top was a golden eagle. I dare not guess at its value, nor at that of the poles and cords that held up the silken walls. Certainly, no monarch on earth could have found sufficient coffers of gold to pay for them, try as he might. And there, within, was a damsel. No flower could match her in beauty, neither the lily nor the first summer rose. She lay on a bed whose cover alone was worth more than a king's castle; but all that she wore on her delicate body was a shift. To shield herself from the sun she had thrown about her a priceless white fur cloak lined with Alexandrinian purple. And, where her skin could be seen, it was whiter than the hawthorn flower.

As the knight stood there the lady beckoned him to sit before her bed. 'Lanval,' she said, 'sweet friend, for your sake I have left my country to find you. I have travelled far; and now, if you prove as worthy and courteous as I believe, no emperor, no great lord or king will ever have felt the joy and happiness that will be yours. For I must tell you that I love you above all things.'

Lanval gazed at her. How beautiful she was. The spark of love in his heart became a burning flame. And this was his reply: 'Fair lady, if it is your pleasure to grant me the great joy of your love, you may ask of me anything that you wish. Whatever it may be, I will seek to do with all the power I have. All others in the world shall be as nothing to me. My heart shall be entirely yours. Never shall I leave you; this is my whole desire.' When the damsel heard these words, all doubts disappeared, and love grew between them. Now Lanval was in luck at last! The lady gave him a magical gift: that however much he spent or gave away, he would never have any less. It was a joyful boon! The more he spent of gold and silver, the more he would possess.

Then said the lady, 'Dearest friend, there is one thing I must ask, beg and indeed command you: not to reveal our secret to a single soul. I tell you, without any waste of words, that if our love ever is known, you will lose me forever. You will never be able to see or find me again.'

He replied, 'Have no fear; whatever you wish or command shall be done.' Then he sat down beside her and they spoke of many things and rejoiced in each other's company.

But, as darkness fell, she said, 'Beloved, the time to leave has come. I shall remain here. But listen, I have one thing more to tell you. Whenever you wish to speak with me; whenever you long for my company, and have in your mind some secret place where lovers can meet without harm or dishonour, I shall come at your bidding. No one but you will be able to see me; no one shall hear my voice.'

Lanval's heart grew light at this promise. He kissed his dear damsel and rose from the couch. The maidens who had taken him to the tent now came and brought him rich and splendid clothes. In these he seemed the handsomest knight on earth and the most courtly too. The ladies gave him water to wash his hands in the golden bowl and a soft towel to dry them;

then they brought him food – ah, what a feast, so fragrant, so delicious – all the more so since he took it with his lady. How sweet it was to kiss her when he willed, and to hold her in his arms.

When they had risen from the table, the knight's horse was led to him, newly saddled, with rich and noble trappings; a prince could not have asked for better. His farewells said, Lanval rode away towards the city, often looking behind him. He was troubled and perplexed. What a strange adventure! Was it a dream? Surely it could not be true. But when he reached his lodging he found that his men were all in the finest new apparel. It was no dream! That very evening, he invited his fellow knights to a feast. They wondered, of course, how this change had come about, for he had been without any means at all.

Now, though, all was changed. If any knight were in need of shelter, he was invited to Lanval's home and royally treated. Lanval gave splendid gifts; Lanval ransomed prisoners; Lanval gave clothes to wandering minstrels; Lanval did all manner of good deeds. No one, friend or stranger, ever left him empty handed. But what gave him most joy of all was the power to see his lady and have her company, to call her to him, both night and day, as often as he wished.

In the same year, so the story goes, just after the feast of St John, some thirty knights were gathered for sport and pleasure in an orchard garden, just beneath the castle tower in which the queen was staying. Among them was Gawain, so too was his cousin, the fair Ywain. Then Gawain, that flower of knights, loved by all, spoke to the company. 'In God's name, lords,' he said, 'we treat our comrade Lanval villainously. He is so generous and noble in his behaviour – he is, you know, the son of a mighty king – yet we have not even brought him with us today!' So several of them at once went back to Lanval's lodging and persuaded him to come.

Up above, at a window carved out of the stone, the queen was sitting with three of her ladies. As she looked down at the gathering of knights, she noticed a less familiar face. Surely that was Lanval, the lone one, not often seen at court. She told one of her ladies to summon the most elegant and beautiful of her damsels to accompany her to the garden; they might join there in the merrymaking. Some thirty maidens were called together and, as they came down the steps, the knights stood waiting to give them a joyful welcome. They took the maidens by the hand, one and one, and exchanged sweet talk, never forgetting, of course, the rules of courtesy.

Lanval stayed apart, away from the rest. He was longing to see his own loved friend, to hold her in his arms. What pleasure could he take in watching the courtship of others? But there was one who perceived him sitting alone – the queen, none other – and she went straight towards him, and sat down by his side. Then she revealed to him what was in her heart. 'Lanval,' she said, 'I have long honoured and loved you. I see that none of my maidens has the power to please you, and this is well. For I say to you now that I am entirely yours; may this also be *your* desire. Are you not glad? You should rejoice at this gift.'

'Lady,' he replied, 'you must let me be. I have no thought of loving you. I have long served the king; never will I betray him or his trust.'

The answer inflamed the queen with rage, and in her wrath she spoke rash words. 'Lanval,' she said, 'I see that you do not care for the love that I offer you – indeed, for any woman. Where do you take your pleasures? Coward! Villain! Evil man! What a misfortune for my husband to have allowed you in his court!'

Lanval was aghast at her rage and, in his haste to answer, he said a thing that he was long to regret. 'Queen, I have no knowledge of the matters you speak of. I love and am loved by a lady who in all ways outmatches all others in the world. Why, any one of her servants, even the lowest, is worth more than you, madam queen, in beauty of face and person, in wisdom and goodness both!'

The queen rushed to her room in tears, shocked and horrified. How could such terrible things have been said to her! How dared the knight humiliate his queen! She took to her bed, letting it be known that she was ill. To herself she vowed that she would never rise again until the king, her husband, avenged her wrongs and brought the offender to justice.

That evening Arthur returned after a pleasant day in the forest, and entered the queen's apartment. At once she fell at his feet and begged him to listen. The knight Lanval, she said, had insulted and humiliated her. He had asked for her love, and, when she refused, had boasted of another so distinguished, such a marvel that the least of her servants, the poorest kitchen maid, was more noble, more lovely, more gracious than the queen. Anger seized the king; he swore that if the knight could offer no true defence in court, he would be burned or hanged. Then he left the queen and summoned three of his barons, telling them to arrest Lanval and bring him into his presence.

But what of Lanval? He had returned to his lodging in a state of anguish and despair. He had lost his most dear lady by revealing the secret of their love. Alone in his room he called to her again and again; but to no avail. He cried out in torment; he fell in a swoon, came to, and swooned again. A hundred times he begged her to have mercy, to speak – if only a single word. He cursed his unwise heart and blabbing mouth. It was a wonder that he did not kill himself. Yet for all his cries and moans he could not break the damsel's silence; all his pain and torment could not move her; she answered never a word. The gift had been taken away. Ah, Lanval, what will become of you?

The barons came to his door and told him that he must straightway go with them to the court; the king required him to answer the queen's complaint. Lanval rose and went with leaden feet. If they had come to kill him he would have been happier. Death seemed a welcome friend. Silent and downcast he stood before the king; you could not doubt his anguish and despair. The king spoke with a cold anger. 'Vassal,' he said, 'you have done me great wrong. You have foully tried to bring shame on your king and dishonour to the queen, and you will have cause to regret your deed. What folly to boast as you did of this unknown lady! She would have to be more than human if her very chambermaid outmatched our queen in beauty and in worth.'

'Sire,' said Lanval, 'at no time, either by word or deed, wish or intent, have I brought dishonour or shame to you or your house.' Then, point by point, he answered the queen's attack. He had never sought her love; he had never pursued unknightly ways. But in one thing he had been wrong – to boast to the world of his lady, and his words had lost him her love, though they were true. 'Now all my hope is gone,' he ended, 'I have no wish to live. Whatever is ordained, I shall accept.'

The king was still enraged but, to give weight to his judgment, and so that none should think him hasty and unfair, he sent for his advisers to discuss what should be done. Whether they liked it or not they had to obey. They decided that a trial was to be held, and for this they chose a date when the rest of the court would be present, not only the councillors. Lanval was to give pledges that he would appear on the appointed day. Then they brought these decisions to the king.

But how and where was Lanval to find these pledges? He was a stranger, lost and bewildered, far from his own land and family. Then Gawain came forward, offering to stand bail, and one by one the other knights followed him. 'Very well,' said the king. 'I accept you as sureties. But the pledge – for each man separately – is everything that you hold from me, lands, fiefs and all.' A hard bargain!

But each man gave his word. And, when this was settled, Lanval returned to his lodging. The knights, you may be sure, took care to go with him, scolding him pleasantly. 'You are a foolish fellow! Be more cheerful. Forget this accursed love affair! Down with all love affairs! They are a web and a trap.' Every day they went to see him – was he eating and drinking properly? A worse fear was that he might harm himself, or go out of his mind. It was an anxious time for those knights, I can tell you. They were not sorry when the day of the trial arrived.

And now the day had come. The king and queen took their place; the barons were already assembled, and the guarantors brought in Lanval. All the knights grieved for him. There were at least a hundred who would have done everything in their power to get him released straight away; they knew that the accusations were false. The charge and defence had been set before the court, and now the verdict lay with the barons. Many of them were troubled at the plight of this well-born knight from a distant kingdom, now in such danger of his life. Others, though, hoped to win favour from the king by judging Lanval guilty.

At last the Count of Cornwall rose and spoke. 'We must perform our task correctly; whatever our personal views, right must prevail. The point is this. The king has accused his vassal – I heard you call him Lanval – of a grave misdeed. He is charged with an offence arising from a boast made about a lady, a boast which has enraged the queen. No one is accusing him but the king, and I have to admit that, if it were not that one should honour one's lord in all things, there is really no case to answer. The king must accept our ruling, since he laid the matter in our hands. I propose that we put this Lanval on oath. If he can give proof of his claim; if the lady comes forward and those words that the queen resented are shown to be true, he will be acquitted, since he did not intend to insult the queen, only to state a fact. But if he cannot give proof, then he must leave the king's service and be banished from our fellowship of knights.'

Lanval then was told that he should ask the lady to come in person to give credence to his case. But he replied, 'Impossible. I would never ask her to come nor have I any right to do so.' When the messengers brought back this answer to the judges, it seemed as if Lanval were doomed. Moreover, the king was urging them to hasten; the queen's impatience was very hard to bear.

What could the judges do? They were just about to give their verdict when they saw two maidens of striking beauty riding towards the court, each on a finely accoutred palfrey, and each of them wearing a close-fitting dress of a violet colour. They were a pleasure to behold. Gawain and three other knights went at all speed to Lanval and told him of the happening; they begged him to look at the maidens; one of them might well be his lost friend. But Lanval said that he did not know them; he had no idea where they came from or where they were going. Still, the maidens rode on until they reached the dais where Arthur was sitting. There they dismounted. Ah, they were lovely, those damsels! They addressed the king in courtly fashion but without subservience, saying, 'King, we pray you, have rooms made ready, with silken hangings, for our lady's coming. She desires to lodge in your palace.' The king readily granted their request and sent two knights to conduct them to the royal guest rooms above. There, for the moment, we leave them.

Then he demanded the barons' verdict. 'Tell them,' he added, 'that I am greatly angered by their delay.' But they replied that they had not yet come to a decision. And since the ladies' arrival, they needed further time. So they gathered together again, but full of unease. The courtiers were increasingly restless; their murmurings grew louder every minute. The judges felt that a verdict must be reached. Yet just at that moment two even more remarkably handsome damsels on fine Spanish mules came riding along the street, superbly dressed in clothes of Phrygian silk. A joyful sound rose from the waiting crowd: 'Lanval is saved!' 'Rescue has come!' 'Lanval the brave!' 'Lanval the good!' – and more of this kind.

Gawain and the other knights once again hastened to Lanval. 'For the love of God, speak!' they cried. 'Two more damsels have come, each of incredible beauty. Surely one of them is your lady.' But Lanval, after the swiftest glance, said that he did not know them and certainly did not love them. What was to be done with the sullen fellow?

As for the ladies, they rode right up to the king, and then dismounted. The courtiers gazed at them with admiring eyes; you could hear their murmurs of praise on every side. All agreed that in beauty of face, of person, they far outshone the queen. The older of the two, courtly and wise in manner, now addressed the king, as one of high birth to another: 'King,' said she, 'I trust that you have the royal apartments prepared for the coming of my mistress; soon she will be here to speak with you.' The king directed that they should be taken to join the other two damsels. Then, when they had gone, he summoned the barons to give their judgement; he would tolerate no more lingering. Too much of the day had gone, and the queen's vexation and wrath were more than he could endure.

But what was this? All eyes turned, as a maiden on a white palfrey appeared, riding towards the court. In all the mortal world, no one could ever have matched her beauty. Her horse, likewise, so highbred, gentle and elegant, could have had no earthly rival of its kind. So rich were its trappings that the greatest monarch could not have purchased them except by pledging all of his lands, and more. The lady wore a snow-white tunic, the lacing on each side revealing her white skin. She was like a sapling tree; her face a white camellia; her eyes were stars, her nose, her mouth – but you must imagine these. A golden thread does not shine as brightly as the light thrown from her hair, which fell in waves about her. She wore a cloak of lustrous silk, its long folds reaching the ground. On her wrist was a sparrow hawk; behind her followed a greyhound. In the whole town there was no one, rich or poor, old or young, who did not gaze with wonder and with awe. No one jested; no one spoke at all. The judges were as dazzled as the rest.

She approached the court without haste. Those who loved Lanval went to him once again, to tell him of the maiden; her coming would most surely deliver him. 'Lord and comrade,' they said, 'a lady has journeyed here. Her hair – it is neither red nor brown. Her face – well, she is simply the most

beautiful of all women in the world.' Lanval listened and raised his head. He knew this lady.

Then he sighed. The blood rushed to his face and he spoke quickly. 'In God's name,' he said, 'that is my beloved. If she has come to condemn me, I am ready to die. Yet a moment's sight of her will mend my sorrows.'

The lady entered the palace; no such marvel of beauty had ever been within those walls, nor would be again. When she reached the king she dismounted and dropped her cloak. All watched her, spellbound. The king stood at her coming, as one monarch meeting a greater one. Barons, knights and courtiers – all desired to serve her, in however humble a fashion. But the lady had no wish to linger. 'King,' she said, 'I have loved one of your vassals, Lanval – you see him there. He spoke words which brought him to trial, and is now in danger of death. I do not wish him to come to harm. You should know that the queen spoke falsely; he never sought her love. As for the boast he made; if my presence here can help the verdict in his favour, then be it so; the barons can set him free.'

The king said, 'Let the judges speak, in accordance with the law.' Not one of them had any further doubt, and Lanval was a free man. The lady turned to leave, with her retainers. Much as he desired, Arthur could not make her stay. Outside the hall was a great piece of marble, used as a mounting-block by heavily armoured men. Lanval stepped on to it; when the maiden came out on her palfrey, he leapt in a single bound on to its back, behind her. Together they rode to Avalon (so the Breton legends tell),

to that loveliest and most secret of islands. There the lady took her handsome knight. No lays have told what happened after, so there my tale must end.

So with the lady he has gone
To the fair isle of Avalon.
No one has heard what there befell.
Knowing no more, no more I tell.

The Two Lovers
LES DEUS AMANZ

n Normandy there is a high mountain. Right at its very peak is the tomb of two young people, a boy and girl. One of the Breton lays tells the extraordinary tale of how this came about; a tale of how, long, long ago, two young lovers met their deaths in the strangest way by reason of their love. The lay is known in English as the lay of 'The Two Lovers'.

At the time when this happened you would have seen a fair and noble city beside the mountain. It had been built by the King of the Pistrians; he had called it Pitres after its people, and the name lives on to this day. Indeed, the region around is still known as the Valley of Pitres. The king had a young daughter, lovely to look at and gifted in courtly ways. She was the only one who could cheer his sadness since the death of his queen, and they were close companions. But now that she was near to marrying age, people felt that she should not always be kept as a child in the palace. Many a young prince wished to be her suitor.

As these whispers reached the king, sometimes through his councillors, he was greatly troubled. How could he seem to agree, and yet still prevent anyone from actually winning his daughter's hand? An idea came to him. He had announcements made in every part of the kingdom that whoever wished to marry his daughter must pass a certain test: he must carry her in his arms to the top of the mountain towering over the town. Furthermore, during the climb he must not pause to rest, even for a moment. 'Do not dare to question the test,' the king declared. 'It has long been ordained and destined.'

As soon as the news became known, plenty of hopeful suitors arrived to try the climb. It should be easy enough, they thought. But it was not, and every one of them failed. A few of the most determined managed to reach about halfway up the mountain side, but the effort left them almost dead of exhaustion; they could certainly get no further. The supply of suitors dwindled; the girl remained unmarried, and this pleased the father well.

Yet who can be safe from Chance? Among the nobly-born young men in that country was one especially handsome, brave and courteous; a count's son, who strove to be first in everything that he did. King and courtiers liked him well when he came to serve at the palace. But while there one day he saw the king's daughter, and his heart was lost. He begged her to accept his love, and if she were able, to grant him hers in return. How could she resist so noble and charming a lover – and one whom her father also valued? And when she told him that she not only allowed him to love her, but that her heart was lost to him also, his joy could find no words. 'Nothing can divide or end our love,' said one to the other and this proved so.

But they had to hide their feelings from the prying eyes of the court. Only in secret could they meet and speak. They could scarcely endure their suffering – but the young man wisely said, 'Sweet friend, it is better to wait in patience than to betray ourselves and lose all. The risks are far too great.' Yet even reason and caution can wear thin, and a time came when his anguish broke through both. 'Sweet damsel,' he said, 'I cannot endure being separate from you any longer. I beg you to steal away from the court with me. Your father will never let you go unless I carry you right to the mountain peak – and no man has ever reached it yet, even when climbing alone and carrying nothing.'

The girl said, 'True, no man is strong enough for that journey. Yet my father is dear to me, and if I were to leave him secretly he would lose all wish to live; every day that remained to him would be a torment. But I have another thought. A rich and learned aunt of mine lives in Salerno; she has

studied there for more than thirty years. She is skilled in medical matters and knows the special powers of many herbs and roots. I will write a letter about our difficulties and you will take it to her. She will be able to make you a potion that gives you a strength greater than that of any mortal man. When this is done you must journey back and ask my father for my hand in marriage. He will probably say that you are too young; he will remind you of the conditions laid down. You will answer that you are ready to undertake the test.'

On hearing this, the young man's spirits at once revived. He asked the damsel's leave to start straightway on the journey, and this she gave. First, he went to his home region, and with great speed gathered together rich clothes, gold coins, palfreys and pack horses. As companions he took with him only a few close friends and trusted servants. Then he set forth for Salerno, to seek out the damsel's aunt.

The lady gave him courteous welcome, studied the letter carefully and asked him many questions, then kept him in her house while she worked out what best to do. Meanwhile, she gave him strengthening medicines to increase his power of endurance. At last she handed him a little phial, saying, 'Now young man, the potion I am giving you is of a rare kind, and immensely strong. However tired or downcast you may be, the moment that you drink it you will be entirely refreshed and restored, you will feel new and invincible.'

The young man took the phial and carried it carefully to his home. Then, travelling light for better speed, he made his way to the court and asked the king for his daughter's hand. 'Boy,' said the king, 'you cannot be serious. You have no idea what you are asking.'

'Sire,' said the young man, 'I have given the matter much thought. I am prepared to undertake the test and carry her to the very top of the mountain.'

'As you will,' said the monarch. 'Yet it seems to me a sad business that so young a man should take this risk when so many valiant fellows, older and stronger than you, have failed. Still, what will be will be.'

He appointed a day for the venture and summoned all his courtiers and his vassals to attend. There was no lack of other witnesses, for people flocked from all parts of the kingdom. Everyone seemed concerned for the young pair: would this boy succeed where all the others had failed? The girl herself so longed for him to triumph that she fasted night and day; the thinner she became, the less would be his burden.

And now the great day dawned. Crowds had already gathered in the meadow by the Seine, where they could best watch the ascent. The young man arrived early and alone, the little phial held closely in his hand. Presently, the king led in his daughter. She wore no rich clothes, only a simple shift, and the young man lifted her easily, starting at once up the lowest mountain slopes. He had given her the little phial to carry – but so reckless and excited was his mood that he seemed not to care whether he had it or not. Briskly climbing, he was soon at the halfway mark – the furthest distance that any other had reached. He did not even realize how much the effort had cost him, but the damsel knew. 'My love,' she said, 'the hardest part is before you. I beg you to drink the potion now; you need its help.'

The young man answered, 'Beloved, my heart feels strong. If I stop, even to swallow this potion, the people will shout, "He is failing!"; they

will distract me and I shall be lost. I must not stop.'

Presently, he reached a point two thirds of the way, but he was greatly exhausted; his legs almost failed him; a whirling filled his head. 'Beloved, drink this potion,' begged the girl. But he staggered on, as if he did not hear. At last – there was the summit. He seemed to be at the highest place in the world. But he felt such pain and weakness that he fell to the ground, and never rose again.

The young girl thought that he had fainted, and knelt down by his side, trying to make him drink from the little phial. But his life had gone from his body. When she realized this she uttered loud lamenting cries, and threw down the tiny vessel. The potion sprinkled the mountain side; wherever it fell, year after year sweet flowers and herbs and plants took root and grew.

What became of the maiden? You may ask; I shall tell you. Now that she knew that the boy was dead she was overwhelmed with grief. She lay down beside him, took him in her arms and kissed him again and again on his eyes and mouth. Her sorrow pierced her heart, and she too died, that most noble and lovely of maidens.

Far below, the king and his company waited for the young pair to return. After a time of growing fear, they too began the hard ascent. When at last the monarch saw the lovers, cold in death, he fell down in a swoon. As his senses returned he began lamenting loudly; and all around joined in with anguished cries.

For three days the dead boy and girl were left as if they slept. Then a marble coffin was brought up the mountain, and they were laid within. All agreed that they should rest in that high place where the mountain meets the sky. The mountain was called the Two Lovers Mountain from that day, and it keeps the name still. And that is the tale just as it came about. Love can bring delight and joy. But love immoderate will destroy.

YONEC

ow that I have begun composing lays, I am eager to set down more of these legends. But the one that especially fills my mind is the tale of Yonec, not least for the strange and marvellous way in which his parents came to meet, and the secret of his birth.

In Britain long ago there was a rich old man, lord of Caerwent. The city where his castle stood was by the river Duelas, in those days a thoroughfare for ships. As the old man's years increased, he wished to have some heirs for his wealth and property and so he took a wife. She was a highborn maiden, gifted, courteous and lovely. But all this did her no good. So jealous was the husband of sharing her charm and beauty that he hid her away under lock and key in a large room in a tower. He had a sister, an elderly widow, and he made her the lady's guardian. He was taking no chances! There were some waiting women about, I believe, in another part of the tower, but the lady would not have dared to speak to them, alone, and without permission.

For seven years she endured this sad way of life. She had no children, and she was not allowed to see either friends or relatives. The old man's suspicions ran deep, almost to madness. Thus, when he went to the lady's room at night, no servant, high or low, would have dared to go ahead of him with a candle. Endlessly weeping and sighing, the lady became so downcast that she began to lose her beauty, nor did she take any care for her clothes and looks. You can hardly be surprised! She wished that death would take her, and she did not mind how soon.

Spring came, and the month of April, when the birds fill the air with song. One morning the husband rose very early and prepared to set out for the woods; as always, he made his sister get out of bed and lock the door behind him. The old woman returned, and went to get her psalter, to recite some psalms. The room filled with sunlight, but the lady lay awake weeping. When she saw that she was alone, she began to lament aloud. 'Woe is me,' she said, 'that ever I was born. My lot is hard indeed. Here am I, a prisoner in this tower, and only death can ever set me free. What does he fear, that jealous old man, that he keeps me in this cage? He behaves like a madman, always thinking that he will be betrayed. Yet I cannot even go to church, or hear the holy service. If only I could talk sometimes with other people, if only I had something to divert me now and then, I might put on a friendly face for him, however little I feel it in my heart. Cursed be my parents, and all who handed me over to this monster. They chained me to a jealous dotard and I cannot break the chain. Oh, will he never die! I used to hear many a tale of magical happenings in this country: of wondrous rescues of those in trouble, held against their will; of knights who found fair maidens and loved them truly; of ladies finding worthy lovers, young and valiant knights, handsome and courteous, the flower of chivalry. If such things once were possible, might they not be now? God grant that such good fortune comes to me!'

No sooner had she said these words when something darkened the narrow window; the shadow, it might be, of a mighty bird. Then the bird itself flew into the room; on its feet were leather thongs; it seemed to be a hawk of about five moultings. It alighted before the lady, paused for a while as if to say, 'Look at me well; have no fear!' – and then it turned into a fair and courtly knight.

The lady was amazed. She trembled; she was afraid. First she turned red, then pale; she covered her face. But the knight spoke to her, gently and courteously. 'Lady,' he said, 'you have no cause to fear. The hawk is a noble bird. True, it has certain mysteries, but they need not trouble you. You are safe, be sure of that. I have come to be your devoted knight, and in the hope that you will accept me in return. I have loved and desired your goodwill long and faithfully. No other lady has had my heart, nor ever will. But I could not leave my country and come to you until you had uttered the wish yourself. You have spoken the very words. Now I am here and I offer myself as yours.'

The lady's dread disappeared. She uncovered her face. 'Sir knight,' she said, 'I will accept your love, and return it too, provided that you give a proof that you believe in God, for that will give a blessing to us both.' Indeed, the knight was of such astonishing beauty that her heart was already lost.

'Lady,' he said, 'you are right to ask me this. I want no doubts, no guilt to touch our love. Yes, indeed I believe in the Creator, the bringer of life and light to sinners, who freed us from the sorrow caused by Adam. Send for your chaplain; tell him that sickness has come upon you, that you wish to hear the service for the redemption of sinners. I will by certain magic means take on your appearance and receive the redemption in your place. Then you will be sure of my belief.'

'You have spoken well,' she said.

And now he lay down by the lady's side, but he did not touch, nor kiss, nor

seek to embrace her.

Presently the old woman returned, and called to her charge to awake and rise from her bed; she would bring in her clothes. But the lady said, 'I am sick; I beg you to bring the chaplain speedily – I fear I may be dying.'

The old woman said, 'You must endure your trouble. Nothing can be done until your husband returns from the woods. Do I have to remind you that no one but myself is allowed into this room?'

The lady was much perplexed; what could she do? She cried out, and made a pretence to fall into a swoon. Alarmed, the old woman opened the door and sent for the priest, bidding him come quickly. This he did. So the knight, in the guise of the lady, received the holy wafer and drank the wine from the chalice. Then the priest left, and the woman too, locking the door behind her.

Now the lady and the knight sat beside each other, laughing, teasing, telling each other about their lives. Nowhere could you have found a handsomer couple! At last the knight rose to go, for he had to return to his own country. She begged him to come back soon and to come often. 'Lady,' he said, 'whenever you desire it, I shall be here, before an hour is out. But be cautious and moderate, or we shall be in dire trouble. The old woman spies on you day and night. If she ever discovers our secret she will tell her brother, and in no way will I escape death.'

The knight became a hawk again and took his leave, and now the lady lay in a dream of joy. Throughout the day her happiness grew no less. The next morning she declared that she had recovered entirely. She began to study her looks and clothes, and soon her beauty returned. No longer did she fret at her solitude; she even seemed to enjoy her prison walls. Well, I need not tell you why. Whenever her aged husband left the castle, to hunt or on other affairs, she could take delight in her lover's company. Night and day, early or late, he was there at her calling; who would not wish them joy! But her husband did not fail to notice her radiant looks, the return of her youthful loveliness. Stung by doubts, he asked his sister if she knew any reason for this change. The old woman could not help him. 'What can I tell you, brother? Not a soul is able to speak to her other than myself. And who could ever get through those locked doors? It is strange, though, now I think of it, that she seems so willing to left on her own.'

The lord replied, 'Hm, you have told me more than you know. Now, there is something you must do. In the morning, when I have left and you have locked the doors, pretend to go outside and leave her on her own. But hide in a secret place. Keep watch; you may discover what keeps her in such cheer.'

Alas, the luck of the lovers had gone entirely. Three days later, the old man declared that he must leave on a journey. He had been summoned by the king, he said, but he would be back quite soon. He then went from the lady's room, closing the door behind him. The old woman also seemed to go, but stayed and hid behind a curtain, to see what she might see.

The lady lay as if sleeping, but in truth she was sending a wish for her friend to come straight away, and this he did. Great was their joy at being together, exchanging words and looks of love, until the day was bright and the knight was obliged to leave. The old woman watched and was struck with astonishment and fear, for the man seemed at one moment a man and at another a hawk. When her brother returned – he had not been far away – she told him the strange story. Shocked and enraged, the old man made swift plans. He had iron prongs forged, with razor-sharp points. Then he had barbs cut into them and set the foul contraption in the window space through which the knight came and went. If only the young man could have known of the terrible trap!

Next morning, the old man rose very early – it was not yet daybreak – and said that he was off for a day's hunting. The sister went to see him go, then returned to her bed to sleep. The lady, though, was awake, longing to see the one she loved so dearly. Now she sent him a message that she was alone; they could have several hours undisturbed. As soon as the wish arrived, he lost not a moment, but hastened on, and sped towards the window. But he did not see the spikes. One of them pierced his side and the red blood flowed from the wound. The lady was distraught. He said to her, 'For love of you I am losing my life. It is as I foretold; your very looks would betray us, and bring us doom.'

When she heard these words, the lady fell into a swoon, and seemed as if she were dead. As life returned, her lover spoke to her tenderly, telling her not to grieve; she would be having his child who would comfort her, and would grow in time to be a valiant knight. Yonec would be his name; he would avenge both parents; he would destroy their enemy. 'But now,' he said, 'I can remain no longer. I am in great pain.' Indeed, blood still flowed from his wound. And so he left. But the lady would not stay behind; leaping down from the tower she set out to follow him. It was a miracle that she was not killed, for she leapt from a height of more than twenty feet! Wearing nothing but her shift she followed the trail of blood, on and on, until she came to a hill. In this hill was an opening, spattered with blood. He must have gone within. She entered; all was dark, but a straight path led her right through the hill, and out at last, on the further side, into a beautiful meadow. Here too the grass was wet with blood, which caused her still more anguish.

But it gave her a trail to follow, and soon she came to a city, completely enclosed by a wall; within, every single house and hall and tower seemed to be made of silver. On one side she saw forests, marshes and fields; on the other, a curving river, with more than three hundred ships sailing to and from the city. Downstream, she came on an unlocked gate in the wall, and so she entered, and followed the trail to the castle at the centre. She heard no sound;

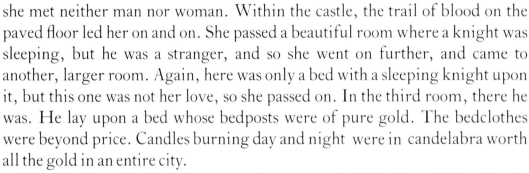

she met neither man nor woman. Within the castle, the trail of blood on the paved floor led her on and on. She passed a beautiful room where a knight was sleeping, but he was a stranger, and so she went on further, and came to another, larger room. Again, here was only a bed with a sleeping knight upon it, but this one was not her love, so she passed on. In the third room, there he was. He lay upon a bed whose bedposts were of pure gold. The bedclothes were beyond price. Candles burning day and night were in candelabra worth all the gold in an entire city.

The lady knew her knight at once, but approached him in such fear that he might be dead that she fell on the bed in a swoon. Her lover clasped her in his arms, lamenting their misfortune. As her sense returned, he tried to comfort her, then gave her serious counsel. 'Sweet friend,' he said, 'in God's name, flee from here. Go, go. I shall die before daybreak. If you are found in this place, you will be in gravest danger. My people know that I meet my death because of my love for you.'

The lady said, 'Dearest friend, I would rather die with you than return to my husband. That would be greater suffering. Indeed, if I did return to him, he would kill me certainly.'

But the knight gave her a ring, saying, 'If you wear this, your husband will remember nothing, nor will he keep you shut away as he did formerly.' Then he also made her take his sword, bidding her to keep it safe for her son; no one else was to touch it. When the boy had grown to be a worthy and valiant knight, she would journey with him and her husband to a feast, held near an abbey, in which was a certain tomb. Here, the son would learn of his father's death, how cruelly he was killed, and the true facts of his birth. And then, being given the sword, he would do what he would do, as she would see.

Last, the knight gave her a long tunic, richly woven, so that he might have fitting wear as she left the castle. 'Now go,' he said. 'Go fast, for time is short.' So she went, with ring and sword; they were a comfort to her. She had gone half a league from the city when she heard tolling bells, and sounds of lament from the castle. Four times she swooned with grief, but at last she made her way to the hill, travelled through and came to her own region. Then she returned to her husband. As the knight had promised, he made no more slanders against her, nor shows of jealousy.

In due time the son was born. He was given the name Yonec, and was brought up in noble ways, and he was loved by all. In the whole kingdom you could not have found a more handsome and courteous boy and man. When he came of age he was dubbed knight – but wait! The year had strange events, as you shall hear.

In the manner of the time, when the feast of St Aaron was celebrated in Caerleon and several other cities, the lords of the region were summoned to attend. Among them was the husband of the lady. Dressed in his richest clothes, and taking with him his wife and son, he prepared to go, but since they were unsure of the way, a youth offered to be their guide. He led them along a road until at dusk they came to a castle, fairer than any in the world. In its grounds was an abbey, and the young squire asked the holy people if they might provide a lodging for the night; thereupon husband, lady and son were welcomed in. They were looked after well and with special honour in the abbot's guest-chamber. Next morning, after mass, they were about to leave when the abbot came to talk to them, and begged them to stay awhile; he wished to show them the dormitory, the chapter house, the refectory, and other parts of the place. And, since they had been so kindly received, the lord agreed to stay.

After they had dined, they were taken about the abbey. Last, they went to the chapterhouse, and there they saw a great tomb, covered with a richly embroidered cloth, with a wide gold band running through. At the head and feet and at the sides were twenty lighted candles in candelabra of the finest gold. The censers which gave their tribute of fragrance all day long were of amethyst – no honour seemed too much. 'Who lies here?' asked the guests. 'Whose is this tomb?'

The people of the place began to weep, and as they wept they spoke. 'Alas, there lies the flower of knights, none more valiant, more handsome nor more loved has ever been born. He was the ruler of this land, a prince of princes, matchless in courtesy. But he was cruelly brought to his death at Caerwent, because of the love of a lady. Since then we have had no lord, but have waited – as he told us before he died – for the son he was to have by this same lady. We have waited long.'

When the lady heard this tale, she cried out to the young knight, 'Fair son, now you have heard why God has brought us here! In this tomb is your true father – killed most foully by this vile old man. The time has come to give you your father's sword; I have guarded it for this day.' Then, in the hearing of all, she told the tale that you have heard, of the father's coming, of how his death was caused, and all that led to the young knight Yonec's birth. She was never to speak again, for she fell upon the tomb in a faint, but the faint was death. When the son saw that his mother's life had gone, he struck off the head of his stepfather; so with his father's sword he avenged his father and mother both.

When all this became known in the city, the lady was taken up with greatest honour and was buried in the tomb beside her lord. Yonec was made the ruler of that land. And so, in time, this lay was made, to show what sorrow and grief may be endured in the high cause of love.

THE NIGHTINGALE
LAUSTIC

shall tell you of a curious and moving happening that the Bretons made into a lay. 'Laustic' is its name in Brittany; in France they call it 'Rossignol'; the English name is 'Nightingale'.

In a thriving town in the St Malo region there lived two knights, each with his own fortified mansion. Their homes stood side by side, making them neighbours. The renown of the knights was great; indeed, it gave an added distinction to the town itself. One of the two was married to a lady whose charm and understanding were equalled only by her beauty and courtly behaviour. The other knight was a debonair bachelor with a high reputation among his peers for his courage, style, and skills of chivalry. Wherever there was a chance of doing deeds of honour and daring he was sure to be found. He fought in tournaments; he spent and gave with a generous hand, and he loved like a true knight. As it happened, the lady of his heart was his neighbour's wife, of whom you have just heard. So constant was his devotion, so urgent were his entreaties, that she in turn began to love him above all things – and not less either for the praise that she heard about him on all sides. They were also, of course, near neighbours. Yet they knew that the more they loved, the greater was their need to be careful and discreet, never seen, disturbed or suspected. They were able to keep their secret more easily because their homes adjoined, house and hall, cellar and keep. Nothing lay between them but a grey stone wall in the grounds. When the lady stood at her window, she could speak across to her friend and he to her; they could exchange gifts too by tossing them over. Indeed, there was little to spoil their pleasure in this delightful game, and both were happy enough – except for one thing: they could not ever meet and be together. For I must tell you this, the lady was closely guarded whenever her husband was from home. But love made the pair so cunning and so resourceful that they still found ways of exchanging words and looks. After all, what harm could there be in looking out of a casement window?

So for many a month this manner of love continued. A summer came, when all the woods and fields were green and new and the gardens all in flower. Lightly perched on the flower tops the small birds voiced their joy in sweetest song. I tell you truly, the knight and lady took their own good part in

nature's play of love, though they could use no more than words or looks. At night, when the moon was shining and the lady's husband slept, often and often she would leave his side, wrap herself in a cloak and go to the window, knowing that her sweet friend was doing the same. The two would stand communing until dawn. Their joy in these frail exchanges never grew less, especially since anything more was denied to them. But so many times did the lady leave her bed and stand all night at the window that a cold anger filled her husband's mind. 'Why do you leave my bed?' he asked her. 'Where do you go? Speak, lady!'

'My lord,' she replied, 'I go to hear the song of the nightingale. Those who have never yet known that sound have missed one of the marvels of the world. This is why I rise, and stand at the casement. So sweetly does the bird sing each night that I cannot close my eyes. It stirs in me such longing that I cannot hear it enough. Therefore I go to the window.'

When the husband heard these words he gave a scornful laugh, evil and angry, and at once made plans to catch the nightingale. Every squire and page and serving man in his household was ordered to make some trap or snare or net and set it about the garden, until there was no bush or tree, hazel or chestnut, left without snare or lime. Soon the bird was caught, and taken, still alive, to the knight. Ah, what pleasure to feel it in his hands! He went to the lady's room. 'Madame', he said, 'where are you? Come forward and speak with me. I have caught your bird, with birdlime, the one which has kept you awake so often. Now you can sleep in peace; it will never wake you again.'

The lady was struck with grief and dread. 'Husband,' she said, 'I beg you – will you not give me the bird?'

His answer was to kill it before her eyes, spitefully wringing its neck with his two hands. Then he threw the little body at the lady, so that her shift was spotted with blood, and strode from the room. The lady took up the bird, and wept over it long and grievously, cursing those who had set the traps and caused her to lose all joy. 'Woe is me,' she said. 'Misfortune is my lot. Never more can I rise in the night and go to the window and talk with my sweet friend. He will think that I am fickle, or faint of heart. But I know what I must do. I shall send him the nightingale and tell him what has befallen.'

She wrapped the little bird in a piece of samite, embroidered in gold with secret signs. Then she called a trusted servant and sent him with the gift and the message to the knight. The knight took the little package, listened to the messenger's tale, and shared the lady's grief. But he acted as he should, in knightly fashion. He had a little casket made, not of iron or steel but of pure gold, set with rare and beautiful jewels. He placed the nightingale within, and carefully covered it over. Then he had the casket sealed, and carried it with him all his days.

This happening could not long be hidden. The Bretons wrote a lay about it; 'Laustic' is its name, and here you have heard its story.

MILUN

ow shall I tempt you to read this tale? You will not regret it, I promise you. New way or old way of telling, the story is the thing, and this is no ordinary story. First, I shall set forth briefly how it all came about, and where, and why.

Milun was born in the southern part of Wales. From the first day of his knighthood no opponent could ever unhorse that young man. What a hero he was, so noble and courtly, yet so valiant and strong in battle! His fame travelled far beyond his own region, reaching Ireland, Norway and Gotland as well as England and Caledonia. He was envied by many but loved by more, and was honoured even by princes.

Now in Milun's homeland lived a certain nobleman with a lovely and gifted daughter. She had heard much about Milun, and had quite lost her heart to the knight. At length she sent him a message, saying that if he wished, she would be his true love. Milun knew of her grace and beauty, and he was delighted. He said to the messenger, 'Tell the damsel that I thank her deeply for her offer, and that, as a true knight, I offer her in return all of my love and loyalty.' Then he gave handsome gifts to the young man, and promised him his protection and goodwill. 'Good friend,' he said, 'I ask you to do your utmost to arrange a secret meeting between the damsel and myself. But remember: no one must ever learn of it. Now take her this gold ring and tell her that whenever she desires to see me, she has only to send word, and I shall come.'

The messenger returned to his mistress, told her all that Milun had said, and gave her the gold ring. Ah, what joy she felt. And so Milun and the highborn damsel came to know one another. Their meeting place was an enclosed garden that the lady could enter from her chamber. It was as if they could never have enough of each other's company, but they could not marry, as the lady's father had promised her to a wealthy nobleman of the region. Then a day came when the damsel realized that she was to have a child. She was distraught; she wept and wrung her hands. 'Woe is me!' she cried. 'If this is known, my honour and my good name are lost forever. The punishments are harsh; I shall be tortured, or sold to be a slave in a foreign land.' For in certain parts that was indeed the custom.

Milun sought to comfort her, and at last a plan was agreed upon. 'When the child is born,' the lady said, 'you must take it to my married sister in Northumbria. She is both rich and wise, and has good understanding. I will give you a written message explaining why you have come. You will also tell her in your own words that this is her sister's child and the cause of much anguish. Say that I trust her to see that the child, whether a girl or boy, is brought up in seemly fashion, trained in the ways of honour and courtesy. I shall hang this ring – your gift to me – around the child's neck, and add to it a letter. In it I shall tell both the father's name and the mother's sorrowful story. When the child is fully grown and has reached the age of reason, it should be given the letter and the ring, both to be kept carefully until parent and child meet again.

The damsel had an old woman attendant who had been her nurse as a child. 'Old nurse,' the damsel said, 'you must help me now.' And she told of her trouble. So well did the old woman shield her from gaze or question that no one suspected her condition, and in due time she gave birth to a baby boy. Then the damsel and the old woman hung the ring around the child's neck, and a silk purse holding the letter, hiding them well beneath the infant's wrappings. Then they laid the child in a cradle on a white linen sheet. Under its head they placed a pillow of silken softness. Over all was an embroidered coverlet, edged with marten fur. Then the old woman lifted the cradle with the sleeping child, and took it to Milun, who was waiting in the garden with loyal servants, all prepared for the journey to Northumbria.

They left before the dawn; in the darkness nobody saw them leave. Seven times a day they rested as they went so that the infant might be fed and bathed. But they took the straightest path they could, and in good time they reached the sister's castle, and handed over their charge. When the lady had read the letter and heard the story, and knew whose child it was, she accepted it gladly and loved it tenderly. The letter and ring were put by until the right moment came; the bringers returned to their own region, and the secret was not betrayed.

Now Milun left the land of Wales. He crossed the seas and rode out to seek fame on every field of battle. But the damsel remained at home and, presently, her father made arrangements for the wedding. The bridegroom was a man of great power and high reputation, but the lady was filled with grief for her vanished lover and with dread of the coming marriage. Would her secret come to light? 'Unhappy creature that I am!' she cried. 'What is to become of me? I do not want this husband – and he may not want me. Will he discover my wrong? If so, I shall end my days as a slave. If only Milun and I could have married, the secret would have been ours alone. I live like a prisoner, surrounded by guards and officials, by enemies young and old, who hate to see the happiness of true love and rejoice when it turns to misery. That misery now is mine. If only I could die!'

But die she did not and, after the wedding, her husband took her away to his own palace. There for a time we leave them.

Milun at last returned from the wars. They had brought him glory, but had not cured his love, and he was cast down by grief and despair to find his damsel gone, the wife now of a stranger. Only one thing brought him hope, the fact that her new home was in his region. How could he let her know, in utmost secrecy, that he had returned? He thought long, and an idea came to him. He had a swan which he loved dearly. He wrote a letter, sealed it with his ring, and tied it around the bird's neck, hiding it in the feathers. Then he called for one of his squires, a youth whom he could trust. 'Listen,' he said, 'change your clothes so that your place of service will not be known. Then go with all speed to the castle of my beloved; carry this swan, and be sure that it gets into her own hands. I can rely on you to use your wits.'

Off went the squire, carefully carrying the bird under his cloak. He took the straightest path and swiftly reached the town where the castle lay. At the main gates he called to the porter, 'Friend, I am by trade a bird-catcher. In the meadow by Caerleon I caught a swan, and I wish to present it to the lady of this place. Her goodwill would be useful, you understand, if I am to move freely through this region.'

The gatekeeper said, 'Friend, the lady speaks with no one. Yet – who knows? – it may be possible. I shall see in what mood she is in, then, if a quiet place can be found, away from watching eyes, you can take the bird to her yourself.'

The porter went to the hall and found it empty except for two knights who were sitting at a large table playing a game of chess. He returned to the squire and quietly led him through; deep in their game the players noticed nothing. At the door of the lady's bedchamber the porter stopped. A maiden came out. She heard the squire's errand and directed him to her mistress so that he might give her the bird himself. The lady then called a servant, saying, 'Take the bird; see that it is well looked after and is given plenty of food.'

'Lady,' said the squire, 'this bird is of a rare and noble kind. It is indeed a royal gift and no hands but yours should receive it. You will find it a true companion.' The lady took it into her lap, stroked its feathers – and felt the

secret note. Her blood seemed to turn to ice, for she knew that it was from Milun. She rewarded the bringer, and thanked him well; so he went on his way.

As soon as she was alone she untied the letter and broke the seal. Seeing at the top the name of her beloved she could at first read no further, but sat there weeping, kissing the page a hundred times and more. At last she read what he had written. He told of his grief and suffering, his longing for her, day and night. Yet he had a plan that would allow them to pass messages, one to another. If she could find a plan and time for a secret meeting, she must tell him by letter and the swan would carry it back. 'Give the bird your kindest care,' he wrote. 'Then, when you are ready, keep it from food for three days. Fasten the letter around its neck and set it free. It will fly straight back to its home, my castle, where it knows that it will be fed.'

The lady studied the letter carefully, thought about the contents, then ordered that the swan should be given the best of food and drink and comfort. In this way a month passed.

Listen now to what happened next. By certain wiles and ruses, she managed to secure pen, ink and parchment. Now she could write an answer to her love, and write she did, sealing the letter with her ring. She caused the bird to go without food for three days, so that it would seek its original home, then hung the letter about its neck and set it free. The hungry bird flew swiftly to Milun's castle, and alighted at his feet. Milun felt a thrill of joy. He quickly found the letter, then called a steward, telling him to give great care to the swan and to feed it well.

He thought that he could never tire of looking at the letter, at the damsel's name, at the seal, at the words within. 'Dear friend,' the message ended,

'without you I can have no happiness. Tell me again that this is your thought too, and do so by means of the swan.' So Milun wrote, and wrote again, and the lady wrote and wrote again, and the swan flew bravely between them, their only messenger. It is said that at times they even met. Why should we doubt it? However closely guarded one may be, there is always some crack or crevice to be found, if only now and then. And so passed twenty years.

You may wonder what had become of the young child left in Northumbria. Now you shall know. His aunt, that excellent lady, brought him up in a manner befitting his noble ancestry. A fine young man he was! In due time she dubbed him knight, and when he came of age she gave him the letter and ring, telling him about his parents and the secret of his birth. 'Your father is a most distinguished knight,' she told him, 'bold and valiant; no one in the land has a higher reputation for knightly prowess.' The young man listened with wonder and delight.

He thought to himself: a man born of such a father is a poor unworthy creature if he does not seek his own fame for courage and endurance, beyond the bounds of his own land and region. I have all that I need for the journey, why should I wait another day? And he set forth the very next dawn. His aunt urged him to eat well and behave properly; but as well as scoldings and sage advice she gave him gifts and a large sum of money, wishing him all good fortune.

The young man made for Southampton and set sail as soon as he could find a ship. Soon he arrived at Bonfleur and went on to Brittany. Here he spent freely, fought in tournaments and moved with the richest in the land. No one ever defeated him in combat. Whatever gold he won from the wealthy, he gave to knights in need. He never stayed long in one place, but continued to carry off all the honours and prizes wherever he went. Yet he was always modest and courteous in manner, as befits the best of knights. News of his fame came back to his homeland, where all felt pride in the young man who had gone abroad to seek glory and had gained it so splendidly. No one knew his name for he was always called The Peerless One: the knight without a peer.

Milun too, heard of the young man – how valiant he was, how generous, how none had ever overcome him in battle. I have to say that he did not enjoy what he heard. For while he, Milun, was able to journey from place to place, to bear arms and take part in wars and tournaments, no knight, he felt, should be more valued than himself. He made up his mind to cross the sea and meet this knight in combat; he would humiliate the newcomer; he would prick his

reputation. He would unhorse him, yes, and leave him properly dishonoured. After that, he would go in search of his son. He knew that the boy had left the country, but what after that? Where he was, or what he did, Milun had no way of knowing.

But before he set out on these matters, Milun did not fail to ask his lady if she would give him leave to go. In a sealed letter, carried by the swan, he told her of his plans: first to prove that he was still the knight of knights, unbeaten in combat, then to find their son. 'Dear friend,' she answered, 'I rejoice that you are doing what you wish. Not for a moment would I stand in your way.'

So Milun prepared for the journey, crossed the sea to Normandy, then travelled to Brittany, where he had many acquaintances. There he entertained richly and was known for his generous giving. Everywhere, he keenly sought out tournaments. I believe he spent the whole of one winter in Brittany, keeping many valiant knights in his service. Around Easter time, when the tournament season started again, there were mighty gatherings at Mont St Michel. Fighters came from Normandy, Brittany, Flanders, France – but very few came from Britain itself, the island over the water.

Milun was one of these few. He was known and feared as one of the most formidable of all the warrior knights. 'Which,' he asked, 'is that new young champion?' There was no lack of voices to tell him, nor of fingers to point him out. The young man's arms and shield made him instantly recognized, and Milun observed him closely. He was determined that they would meet in combat before the day was out.

The tournament began. Anyone seeking a jousting partner soon acquired one; there were plenty in the ranks. Milun, you may be sure, acquitted himself magnificently and earned resounding praise. And yet – the newcomer knight was acclaimed above all others, even above Milun. No one could match him in the joust. Milun studied his manner of riding, how he held his lance, the slant of the blows he struck. For all his envy, he could not help admiring what he saw; he even enjoyed the sight of so much skill. He placed himself so that he should be the next to meet the young man in combat, and their joust began.

Milun first struck so hard a blow that his lance was shattered. But this did not unhorse his opponent, who, in return, struck back so forcibly that Milun was the one to be unhorsed. But when the young man saw his opponent's white hair and silvery beard beneath the visor, he was greatly troubled. He took the riderless horse by the reins and brought it to Milun, saying, 'Lord, mount your steed. I am most grieved to have acted so discourteously to one so much more in years than myself.'

Milun leapt to his feet – not angered, but seized by a sudden joy. He had seen a certain ring on the young man's finger when he returned the horse. 'Listen to me,' he said. 'For the love of God, tell me your father's name, and your own name. Who is your mother? Keep nothing from me. I have seen much and travelled far; I have been in wars and tournaments in many lands. Yet never has any knight forced me off my horse. You have unhorsed me, yet I feel for you love, not hate.'

The other replied, 'Sire, I shall tell you as much as I know. My father was born in Wales, I believe. His name is Milun. He loved the daughter of a wealthy lord; I was born in secret, and sent to my aunt in Northumbria. There I was brought up and educated. My aunt looked after me well and, when I left to seek my father, she gave me a horse and arms and gold, besides much good advice. I crossed the sea to make my name as a knight. Now I intend to return to my country to search for news of my father. I long to know more about him, and about my mother, too. When I show him this gold ring and other tokens he will know that I am his son; I do not think he would wish to disown me. Indeed, I hope that I will have his love and attention.'

At this point, Milun could no longer keep silent. He gripped the edge of the young man's coat of mail, crying out, 'By heaven, my life is whole at last.

In truth you are my son. It was in search of you that I left my land this year.' The other waited to hear no more, but leapt from his horse; father and son embraced each other with mingled joy and tears. The very onlookers wept for joy at the sight.

The tournament ended at nightfall and Milun took his son to his own lodging, where they might speak at leisure and learn more of one another. There seemed no end to their delight in hearing each other's story. Milun told of his love for the boy's mother, how her father had given her in marriage to a rich nobleman in that region, how their love through all had remained unchanged. Then he described how the swan had become their faithful messenger, carrying letters that they dared not trust to human hands. The son replied, 'Father, I shall bring my mother and you together. First I shall get rid of her husband, then you will be able to marry.'

It was already dawn when they stopped talking and prepared to depart. They took leave of their friends and set sail for England; the voyage went well, for the wind was fair and strong. But listen to this! On their arrival a youth rushed towards them. He was a page from the house of Milun's lady and had been about to set sail for Brittany with a message for Milun. Now he had no need to go. He handed Milun a letter saying, 'Lord, you would do well to go straight to your lady. Her husband is dead, and she is free. She begs you to hasten. I tell you only what you will find in this letter.'

This was amazing news! Father and son travelled night and day until they reached the castle. The lady was enchanted to see her son, so handsome, valiant and noble. They called no kinsmen; they asked no counsel, but married then and there, and the son gave his mother to his father. They lived thereafter in utmost harmony and content.

Out of this tale of loss and finding, of love at last rewarded, our ancestors made a very moving lay. I too have had a rare pleasure in telling the tale, and I wish the same joy to all listeners.

CHAITIVEL

certain lay runs through my mind; you will understand why when you learn its story. First I shall tell you its name, and where it took place. This lay is usually known as 'Le Chaitivel' (in English, 'The Sorrowful One'); but it is also called by some 'Les Quatre Deuls', 'The Four Sorrows'. Which is the truer title you shall yourself discover.

In the city of Nantes, in Brittany, there lived a lady, above all others in beauty, wisdom and courtesy. There was not a knight in that region who, having seen her even a single time, would not have loved and wooed her without end. Well, she could not love them all, but neither did she care to turn them away. Indeed, that would have been neither wise nor mannerly. A woman, however much sought after, should treat all those who offer love with honour and regard even if she has no wish to listen to their pleadings. As I have said, the lady whose story I am about to tell was courted without cease for her beauty and her charm; would-be lovers sighed and yearned for her night and day.

Now in Brittany at this time there lived four knights. I do not know their names, but all were young, nobly born, handsome, brave and generous, and they were admired all through the land. But – ah me! – all four of them loved the lady and for ever busied themselves with valorous deeds to prove it and to win her for himself. The lady too gave serious thought to the matter; yet how could she choose when all had such high qualities? Besides, by choosing one she would lose three, and no joy lay in that.

So to each she showed great kindness, sometimes sending love tokens, sometimes pleasant messages. Each thought himself the most favoured; but the truth was that she could not choose between them. So each knight remained certain that, in good time, he would outdo all the others in the quality of his service, the ardour of his devotion, and in the valour of his combat. Ah, what feats, what deeds of daring were done by those brave boys! Nothing was too much if it would gain the lady's favour, and her heart. As they rode into battle, all four had about them some love token from her hand, a ring, a sleeve, a standard; all of them used her name as a rallying cry. The lady's kindness did not fail, so the flame of hope burned brightly for all four.

But attend now to what befell. One year, after Easter, the city of Nantes proclaimed a tournament. To meet the four dauntless lovers in combat, knights came from many a region, from France, Normandy, Flanders, Brabant, Boulogne, Anjou, from Brittany and from Nantes itself. All came joyfully and in good time, for they wished to be well prepared. But this caused some restlessness, you understand. And on the eve of the tournament a fierce fighting broke out. The four lovers, fully armed, went to the place outside the city walls, and their own knights followed them. But the main interest of the opponents lay with these four, whose ensigns and shields made them unmistakable. Four of the stranger knights were sent against them, two from Flanders, two from Hainault, all fully equipped for combat and afire to join in battle.

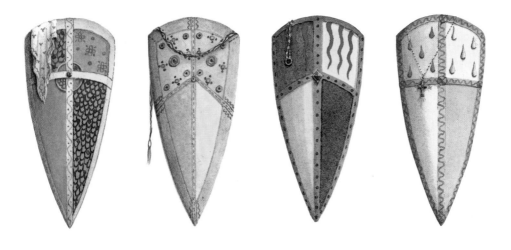

The lovers saw them advance and had no thought of retreat. At high speed, with lowered lance, each one picked his opponent and rode forth. So powerful were the blows that the enemy knights were unhorsed. The lovers did not trouble to catch the horses; they resumed the fight on foot. The followers of their opponents now joined in — it was a furious mêlée. Far around, the air was filled with the noise of jarring blows, the deafening clash of swords. The lady watched from a tower. She could clearly see her own four knights and their men. But all were acquitting themselves so well that she could not in her heart say, 'That one or that one is the most valiant, the one to win my love.'

When the tournament began next day, the ranks of waiting knights pressed thick and close; all were so eager to fight. I cannot tell you how many battles were fought that day outside the city walls. As for the four lovers, they performed so brilliantly that, by nightfall, when the time had come to leave the field, they had carried off all the honours. If only the day could have ended there! But victory made them heedless; they became separated from their followers, and this was to cost them dear. They were taken by surprise; in an attack from the side all were unhorsed; three of the four were killed, and the other gravely wounded. A lance ran right through his thigh.

Now those who had struck the mortal blows were overcome by grief, and threw their shields to the ground. They had not meant to kill these noble adversaries. A great noise and cry rose up from all around; none had ever known so vast a sorrow. The people of the city came out on to the field, all of the warring strangers forgotten. I must tell you that as many as two thousand men undid their visors and tore their hair and beards for grief. Sorrow made them one. Then the four knights, each laid on his own shield, were carried into the city; and there they were taken to the lady of their love.

It was in this way that she came to know of the dire happenings; and the sight made her fall to the ground in a swoon. When she came to herself again, she mourned each one by name. 'Woe is me!' she cried. 'What shall I do? No joy can ever come to me again. I loved these knights, each for his own sake, and they loved me above all things. They were so beautiful, so brave, so noble and generous that I did not wish to lose the others by choosing one, and so I made them compete for my favour. Even now I do not know which to mourn the most. But this is certain: I may no longer disguise or hide my thoughts. What comfort remains for me in this world? Three of these lovely and gifted young men are dead; one is gravely wounded. The dead I shall bury; if the injured man can be cured, I shall give him all the care in my power. The best of physicians will come to him.' Nothing seemed enough to show her love.

The lady had the sick man carried into her own room, then arranged for the others to be prepared for burial. She laid over them rich and noble coverings; she gave a large offering of gold and other gifts to the great abbey where they would lie. And the fourth, who was not dead? Learned doctors were called to the lady's house, and they tended the injured knight until he was healed. The lady came to visit him often and did her best to comfort him. But her grief for the others was with her always; she never ceased to mourn their fate.

One summer day, after dinner, the lady sat conversing with the knight. Then again she was reminded of her sorrow and of its cause, and she bowed her head in thought. He looked at her, perceived that some heavy burden was on her mind, and spoke to her gently. 'Lady,' he said, 'you are troubled. What is in your heart? Tell me. Put aside your grief and let me help you.'

'Dear friend,' she said, 'I was remembering your companions. Never again will a lady, however highborn, however beautiful, gifted, wise, have this chance and mischance, to love and be loved by four such men at once, and then lose them all in a single day – all dead but yourself. And you, too, so sorely wounded, might have died because of my ill-fated love for you all. I wish for my grief to be remembered, and so I shall make a lay about the four of you and call it "The Four Sorrows".'

But when he heard these words, the knight at once replied, 'Lady, make this lay, but you must call it "Le Chaitivel", "The Sorrowful One". Let me tell you why. My three companions have ended their days, their earthly life is over, and their suffering, all the anguish caused by their devotion to you. But I, who escaped the hand of death am bewildered and wretched. I love a certain lady more than anything on earth; I see her always coming and going; she speaks to me morning and evening – yet I am denied the joy of a kiss, an embrace or any exchange but words. Lady, you make me endure so many torments that death would be a blessing. So it is for me that the lay should be named, and that name should be "The Sorrowful One". Whoever calls it "The Four Sorrows" will be changing its true name.'

And so the lay came to be made and was everywhere told and sung. Some of its singers called it 'The Four Sorrows'; you can see why. But the more usual and truer name is 'The Sorrowful One'. Here I come to an end. Whether there is another turn to the tale is not for me to say. I tell you only what I have heard, no more.

THE HONEYSUCKLE
CHEVREFOIL

et me tell you the true tale behind the lay called 'Chevrefoil' and how it came to be made. I have often heard it told, in different ways by different people; I have found it too set down in a written version. But here, as it truly came about, is the story of Tristram and the queen, of their unfailing love, so fine and rare, which brought them so much woe.

Now King Mark of Cornwall was angry with his nephew Tristram because of his love for the queen, and he banished him from the region. Tristram went to his own country, in South Wales, where he was born, and there spent twelve long months. To go back was utterly forbidden. Yet love made him do just this though it meant risking life itself.

Lingering in Wales, he was so downcast and heavy hearted that he broke his exile and made his way to Cornwall to be near the queen. Once there, he passed his days alone, hidden in the depths of the forest, away from human eye. But each evening as darkness fell he would emerge and seek shelter for the night, with peasants or other poor folk. From these, he hoped to learn of the king's comings and goings. They told him what they knew, that the barons had been summoned to Tintagel where the king would be holding court at Pentecost. There would be mighty feastings and celebrations (so they said), and the queen would be coming also.

When Tristram heard this he rejoiced, for the road towards Tintagel went through the forest, and he could not fail to see the queen when she passed. And so, on the day when the king and court would be setting forth, he went to a point in the forest road; there he broke off a hazel branch, split the end into four, carved his name on the side, and stuck the wand in the earth. The queen would be watching out for a sign – they had used this one of a hazel wand before – and when she saw it she would know that her lover was near at hand. He had already secretly sent word that he had waited long in the wood on the chance of seeing her, for without her he could not live. 'We two,' he had written, 'are like the hazel and honeysuckle. When the one has twined round the other, the two grow as one, and thrive and live long together. But if they are torn apart, each dies. Sweet love, so it is with us. Neither without the other can survive.'

The queen rode on her way. She looked at the slope ahead and saw a hazel wand, and the letters carved on it spoke to her. She ordered her escort of riders to halt, saying that she wished to dismount and rest. As soon as they had obeyed her command, she went some distance from the company, calling only her faithful servant Brenguin to wait nearby.

And so, within the wood, in a green bower, away from the trodden path, she found the one who loved her more than any living thing. Their meeting gave them a joy beyond imagining. He spoke what was in his heart, and she did likewise. Then she told him how to seek to be reconciled with the king, who had been greatly troubled at having to banish his nephew. But he had been obliged to do this because of the accusations made against Tristram. Then she prepared to go, leaving him in his solitude. When the moment came of parting, neither could help but weep.

Tristram travelled back by secret paths to Wales, there to pass mournful days until the king his uncle might allow his return. But he was a gifted harp player, and the queen had urged him to make a lay of their story. He thought of the joy of their meeting in the wood, and of the letter that he had written about their love, and he used these to make the lay. 'Gotelef', or 'Goatleaf' is the English name, or sometimes 'Honeysuckle', 'Chevrefoil' the French. And this tale, as I have said, is the truth behind the song.

EQUITAN

he Bretons, I must tell you, had some fine and noble people in those bygone days; they were brave and courtly; many too had special gifts for verse and song. They liked to make lays on the happenings of the time, and so it came about that strange events and characters live to this day in words, when they might have vanished entirely. One curious lay, which stayed in my mind long after I heard it recited, concerns a king called Equitan, ruler and lord of Nantes.

He was a popular monarch, strong and fearless, enjoying sport and pleasures of all kinds. But above all he loved love, the courtly moves of chivalry, the cunning skills and dangers of the chase. Reason has no power in this game of hearts. Luckily he had a seneschal, a brave and loyal knight, who dealt with most of the kingdom's daily business. Government and justice, both, were left in his hands. It was well that he was there, for nothing but the needs of war could make the king forsake his hunting, his river sports or other favoured joys.

This seneschal had a most beautiful wife; though, as you will find, her beauty was to bring misfortune to the land. Truly, in looks and grace, she had no equal anywhere. The king so often heard her praised – her charm, her sparkling eyes, the perfection of her form and face – that he longed to see this wonder for himself. He had practice enough in these matters and soon devised a way to be in her company. He went hunting, alone, in that region, and when evening fell he asked to stay for the night in the seneschal's castle. There he had all the chance he desired to see and speak with his hostess, and to display his own charm and wit. Ah yes, she was even more lovely than he had imagined, most courtly in manner, most pleasant in conversation.

As you might expect, love shot an arrow deeply into his heart. Wisdom, prudence and good sense – what can they ever do against that weapon? His mind became confused and melancholy; he could think of nothing else but the lady. All night long he was unable to sleep or rest. Tossing to and fro, he reproached himself for his folly. 'Alas,' he said, 'what trick of fate has brought me to this region? At the very sight of the lady I am struck by a pain so great that my whole body trembles. What can I do but love her! Yet if I love her I shall be doing a wrong, for she is the wife of my seneschal. He is my faithful friend, and I should be as loyal to him as he is to me. If he were to know of my feelings for her, his life would be destroyed. But if his king were laid low for want of her, would it not be much worse? So beautiful a woman must have love. Her very courtliness is incomplete without the adoration it deserves. How fortunate a man – any man – would be if she were to grant her love. No, no, the seneschal ought not to keep her entirely for himself. He should not mind too greatly if others feel as he does. For my part, I am quite willing to share her with her husband.'

The king gave a deep sigh and lay there, turning these thoughts over in his mind. Then he spoke aloud, 'Why am I so disturbed, so full of doubt? I do not even know if she is willing to accept my love. But I shall soon find out. If she feels as I do, then all my sufferings will vanish. Ah me, the night is long. Will the dawn never come? How many endless hours have passed since I came to this bed last night?'

Morning came at last and, at first light, the king set off for the hunt. But he soon turned back and returned to the seneschal's home, saying that he felt unwell and wished to lie down. The seneschal was greatly troubled, and his wife went to the king's bedside to give what help she could. This was his chance; without delay he began to confess his feelings. 'Lady,' he told her, 'you can bring me life or bring me death. The power is in your hands.'

'My lord,' said the lady, taken aback, 'I must have time to think of what you have said. It is hard to know what to do. You are a king of wealth and power. I am merely the wife of an official. If I were to give you what you ask, you would soon cast me off – and then, where would I be? Love is only of worth between equal partners. The devotion of a man without great possessions but with wisdom and loyalty is of far more value than the passing passion of a king – one who thinks that he has a natural right over his subjects, even in matters of the heart.'

Equitan replied, 'Lady, do not say such things. The men who behave unworthily have no knowledge of courtly behaviour. The

bargaining of merchants has no place in our exchange. A wise and noble lady, who does not easily grant her love, but gives it loyally when it is won, deserves to be sought by the highest in the land and then served with undying love and honour, even if she owns nothing but her dress and cloak. Those who are light and fickle and shift their affections easily will soon be tricked and abandoned in their turn, despised by all. Dearest lady, I offer myself to you entirely. You must not think of me as your king, but as your vassal and lover. I swear to you that everything you ask for shall be given; that every wish shall be to me a command. Ah, lady, do not let me die for want of you. You shall be mistress, I the humble servant; you the proud ruler, I the petitioner.'

The king continued pleading in this manner. He begged so long and passionately for her to end his torment that, at last, her doubts and scruples were swept away; she agreed to love him and to accept his love. To seal this bond they exchanged rings and vowed to keep lasting faith. They kept this vow and loved each other well. In time this love was to bring about their deaths.

For many months no one knew of their love. Whenever they arranged to meet, the king would feign sickness, and give orders that he must not be disturbed. The doors of his room were closed, and even the boldest man would not have dared to enter without being summoned. At such times the seneschal presided over the court, passing judgements, hearing the pleas and plaints. Day after day, week after week, the king's devotion never wavered; he wished for no other woman; he had no desire to marry and would not even discuss the subject. This displeased his courtiers and their angry murmurs reached the seneschal's wife. She was greatly troubled: was she to lose her lover after all? She could not endure the thought.

Usually when they met, the lady was full of joy, kissing and clasping her lover in her arms, but the next time they were together, she wept bitterly, showing every sign of grief. 'Dear love, what is your trouble?' asked the king.

The lady said, 'I weep for the death of our love. You are to take a wife, a king's daughter, and abandon me. I have heard this said, not once but many times; I know that it must be true. Unhappy wretch that I am! Nothing remains for me now but death.'

The king replied, 'Dear love, you need have no fear. I shall never take a wife nor leave you for another. You must take my word for this. Believe me, if your husband were to die, you would be my queen. No one can make

me do otherwise.'

The lady thanked him, joyfully. 'Dear lord and love,' she said, 'if you speak truly, might we not do well to hasten my husband's death? If you are willing to help me, this should not be difficult.'

'Then you have a plan?' said the king. 'As I have told you, whatever you wish shall be done, if it is in my power.'

'Dear lord,' said she, 'if it pleases you, I ask you to come hunting in the forests of my region. You will stay as before in my husband's castle and, on the third day, you will say that you wish to take a bath. You will ask my husband to keep you company. I shall arrange to have the water heated for the two tubs, but the water in my husband's shall be boiling hot – a heat that no man could survive once he had leapt into it. Then, when life has gone,

summon the vassals, both yours and his, and tell them that he suddenly died in his bath, as they may see.'

'What you ask shall be done,' said the king.

Some three months later he announced that he would hunt in the seneschal's region. On the third day he asked for a bath to be prepared. 'You join me for company,' he said to the seneschal, 'and we may speak together.' The seneschal agreed; his lady spoke to the servants, and the two tubs were brought in, each placed before a bed. But the one meant for the lady's husband was filled with boiling water. Now the king came into the room and, finding the lady alone, begged her to sit beside him. This she did, setting one of her maidens to stand guard at the door.

Just then the seneschal returned and was puzzled to find the door closed.

Why did his wife's servant refuse to let him in? Angered, he banged on the door so violently that it burst open. There he saw the king and his wife in each other's arms.

The shock of seeing the husband made the king leap up and jump into the tub, as if to seem that he had been merely taking a bath. But the tub was filled with boiling water, and so he met his death. The wicked plan had rebounded on him, evil returning evil, while the seneschal stayed unharmed. All the long deceit became clear to him; he seized his wife and tossed her head-first into the boiling bath, and so the pair died together. For those who listen to reason, much can be learnt from this tale. Does not love itself lose its virtue and privilege when it draws on the powers of evil?

In any case, here are the facts of the story, just as they took place. The Bretons thought it a worthy theme for a lay, and that is how I came to know this tale of love unwarranted and death deserved.

Eliduc

his tale comes from a very old Breton lay; these are the true facts, I understand, and you must believe them, for strange things happened long ago.

Once there was once a knight in Brittany, a noble and courteous man; no one was braver in battle. Eliduc was his name. His wife Guildeluec was wise and gracious; she was of highborn family, and the two loved each other long and loyally. But a time came when Eliduc had to go further afield in search of military service while his wife remained in Brittany. While away, he met and lost his heart to a maiden, Guilliadun, the loveliest young girl in the kingdom. This was often called the lay of 'Guildeluec and Guilliadun' because it chiefly concerns these ladies; but it is also known as the lay of 'Eliduc'. I shall tell you the facts of the tale.

Eliduc served the king of Brittany, and was a faithful knight to his lord. The king loved and valued him; whenever he was away, Eliduc was left in charge. His valour and skills brought him other privileges. He could freely hunt in the forest, and no forester could prevent him, or even grumble to his face. It was envy of his good fortune, leading to slander and false accusations, that broke his connection with the king. He was banished from the court without knowing why and with no chance of clearing his name, for the king refused to give him a hearing.

Eliduc had no wish to linger; he decided to cross the sea to England – Logres it then was called. He asked his friends to take good care of his wife, and he gave her a promise to love none other while they were apart. Then, with a small company – ten knights in all – he made his way to the coast, crossed the sea, and arrived at the port of Totnes.

There were many kings in the land of England, and endless wars waged between them. In the region near Exeter one ruler had his castle; he was an old man with no male heir. But he had a fair daughter who was now of age to marry. Because he had refused to give her to one of his peers, the rejected lord had declared war on him, and was laying waste his land. He was in sore need of help! Here was Eliduc's chance. He informed the king in a letter that he had come from over the sea and was prepared to fight on his behalf – but if his services were not wanted, he would look elsewhere. The king certainly did want his services. He received the knight and his men with honour and welcome, and arranged their lodging in the house of a wealthy citizen. To show that he was no upstart, Eliduc forbade his men to accept any gift or money during their first forty days in the town.

He had been there three days when a cry went up that the enemy forces were in sight. They had spread through the land and were making for the city gates. Eliduc heard the noise of the frightened crowd, armed himself, and called his men together. There were also forty mounted knights in the neighbourhood, some recovering from wounds. When they saw Eliduc and his company they went to join them. 'Lord,' they said, 'we shall go with you and do as you do.'

Eliduc thanked them, then asked, 'Does anyone know of a narrow pass where we can ambush the enemy? We could await them at the gate but that gives us less advantage.'

One knight answered, 'Lord, in the nearby wood is a thicket with a narrow cart track running through. That is their usual path of return with spoils. It should be easy enough to surprise them there.'

Eliduc replied, 'He who takes no risks makes no gains. You are all vassals of the king, and owe him loyalty, as I do myself. Follow me, and I promise you as few losses as we can help and the chance of winning high repute and glory.'

They showed the path to Eliduc, and he directed them to hide in the bushes, explaining how they were to engage the enemy. The knights struck swiftly; their opponents were quickly routed; many were taken prisoner.

The king meanwhile was in his tower; looking down he thought that Eliduc had abandoned his knights. Moreover, when Eliduc's forces returned, laden with booty, and greater in number than when they had started, he failed to recognize them. He was about to order his men to climb on the walls and shoot them down when a squire arrived on a fast steed. He told how the new soldier had defeated the enemy, how brave he was, how clever. There never was such a knight! He had captured the leader and twenty-nine others, and had destroyed many more.

The king rejoiced and came down from the tower to meet the remarkable knight and give him thanks. Eliduc handed over the prisoners, distributed their arms to his own soldiers, keeping for himself only three fine horses. Everything else he gave away, not only to his own men but to the prisoners.

The king was overcome with gratitude. Need you wonder! For a whole year he kept Eliduc and his followers in his service. He received the knight's oath of allegiance and made him guardian of the land.

The king's daughter, Guilliadun, heard of this brave knight, so noble and generous. She sent her personal chamberlain to request him to visit her, so that they might talk and learn more of each other. Eliduc agreed to come.

The chamberlain went ahead to announce the knight's arrival. Then Eliduc entered the lady's room, and addressed her with charm and courtliness. The girl, he saw, was beautiful. She took his hand, bade him sit down, and they spoke easily of many things. She studied his looks, his manner, and liked them well. She approved, she admired, she began to love. She turned pale, but said nothing to reveal her thoughts.

Presently, Eliduc took his leave and returned to his lodging. He felt sad and pensive and could not understand why. His mind seemed filled by thoughts of the gentle girl who had sighed as she spoke to him. Then he remembered his wife and his promise to keep faith with her.

As for the maiden, now that she had seen the knight she longed for his love. She lay in bed, but could neither rest nor sleep. When at last morning came, she called her trusted chamberlain and told him of her plight. 'I love the new soldier, the good knight Eliduc,' she said. 'I cannot rest for thinking of him. If he wishes to love me truly I am ready to grant him all my love in return. This could bring him good fortune, even the chance to rule this land in time. But if he rejects me, there is nothing for me but grief, and I shall die.'

The chamberlain thought, then offered words of counsel. 'Lady,' he said, 'if you love him so truly, send a messenger with a token – a girdle, ribbon or ring – and ask him to come to you. If he receives your message joyfully, and comes to your asking, these are good signs; you are fairly sure to have touched his heart. Why should you doubt it? No emperor on earth could fail to be glad of your love if you choose to grant it.'

The damsel said, 'How shall I know if the gifts and message are pleasing to him? I should hate him to mock me. But go yourself and study his face as he receives the tokens. Take him a gold ring and my own girdle, and greet him on my behalf.'

The chamberlain left. She almost called him back, but did not do so. While she waited she began to lament. 'Alas, how foolish I am. What do I know of this man from another country? Now I have risked all; if he does not want my love, I am lost for ever.'

Meanwhile, the chamberlain hurried to Eliduc, asked to see him alone, and gave him the tokens and message. The knight thanked him courteously, placed the ring on his finger and tied the girdle round his waist. He offered the chamberlain a gift but the man refused it and returned to the lady. She begged him for news. 'Hide nothing from me,' she said.

The chamberlain answered, 'In my view the knight is skilled at hiding his feelings, but though he said no words, he is wearing both of your tokens. If he did not wish you well he would not take your gifts, let alone wear them.'

But she was not content. 'I must speak to him myself, and tell him how my love for him torments me – but perhaps this will make him flee from me and leave the court for ever.'

'Lady,' the chamberlain replied, 'the king has retained him on oath for a year; so for a year the knight is pledged to serve him. You will have plenty of time and chance to know him and be known.'

This gave the damsel hope. She did not guess that the knight too had his troubles. Since he had first seen the damsel, she had filled his thoughts; nothing else gave him joy or pleasure. Yet before he left his country he had promised his wife that he would love no other woman. Now he was caught in a trap; he wished to be faithful to her, yet he could not help loving the maiden Guilliadun.

The problem seemed beyond him. In despair, he mounted his horse and rode to the castle to speak with the king – but really to catch a glimpse of the maiden.

The king was in his daughter's room playing chess with a knight from over the sea; he was there as the damsel's teacher. The king welcomed Eliduc, made him sit down beside him and said to his daughter, 'Damsel, you should become acquainted with our new warrior and show him great honour. You won't find a better anywhere.' She was glad to hear these words of praise. The knight rose, she took his hand, and they went to sit somewhat apart from the rest.

At first they were silent; neither wished to be the first to speak. But then he thanked her for the gifts she had sent, saying that he had never cherished any possessions more.

She replied, 'I am glad of this. For with those gifts I offer you myself. I would have you for my husband and none other. If this is not to your liking, I shall wed no other man. And now I have freely told you my thoughts, you must tell me yours.'

'Lady,' said Eliduc, 'you do me honour and give me joy. I must tell you that I have agreed on oath to stay one year with the king, then I return to my own country – if you will give me leave.'

The maiden said, 'Beloved, I know that you will not wait until then before

you give me your answer.' They pledged their troth to each other, and spoke no more at that time. But as days went on, the love between them grew.

Meanwhile, Eliduc achieved great triumphs in his work. He captured the king's principal enemy and freed the entire land. His praises sounded everywhere. Fortune smiled on him.

While all this was happening, his own lord in Brittany had sent out three messengers to look for him. He was under heavy attack; his land was being laid waste; he was losing all his castles. 'Why did I let that good knight go?' he lamented. 'Why would I not listen to his story?' Since then he had discovered the truth, and had sent into exile those traitors who had falsely accused the knight, and caused him to leave the land. Now, in his dire need, he summoned Eliduc to come to his aid, calling on his promise of fealty.

Eliduc was much disturbed by the summons, but most of all for the maiden's sake, for he loved her dearly, and she him. There was no folly or sin between them; their love consisted of courting, sweet talk, or exchanging gifts whenever they were together. But it was always the damsel's hope to win him entirely. She did not know that Eliduc already had a wife.

'Woe is me,' the knight said to himself. 'How ill I have behaved. Would that I had never seen this country. Here I have deeply loved a maiden, the king's daughter Guilliadun, and she has loved me. If I leave her, one of us will die, maybe both. Yet I must depart, for my own lord has sent for me, calling upon my oath of fealty. Yes, I must go. Since I have a wife, I cannot marry the damsel of my heart; for Christian law forbids it. Yet parting is so hard. No – whatever blame it brings I am determined not to do harm to my beloved. I shall do as she advises. The king, her father, is no longer troubled by enemies; the land is at peace, so it may be best to depart before the day that ends my allegiance. I shall tell the maiden and ask what she would have me do.'

Having made this decision, Eliduc went straightway to the king, and showed him the letter from Brittany. The king realized that Eliduc meant to go, and he was troubled. He offered the knight rich possessions, treasure and a third of his heritage if he would stay. But Eliduc reminded him that by oath and goodwill he had to help his lord in his distress. He could not refuse. 'But if you need my services again,' he said, 'I shall willingly return with a large force of knights.'

The king thanked him, gave him leave to depart and put at his disposal all the wealth of the castle: gold and silver, dogs and horses, lustrous silken cloths. Eliduc took only a moderate share of each, then asked if he might say farewell to the king's daughter. 'By all means,' said the king. 'That would please me.' He sent a squire to announce the knight's coming, and when Eliduc arrived, she hugged and kissed him at least six thousand times. He began to explain about his departure, but before he could tell the story, or ask what she wished him to do, she turned white as a lily and fainted with shock and grief.

Eliduc cried out; he kissed her and wept and held her in his arms until she recovered. 'Sweet love,' he said, 'let me tell you something. You are my life and death and all my comfort. I come to you because of the pledge between us; but I am obliged by oath to return to my country. I have taken leave of your father, but I shall do whatever you wish, never mind the consequences.'

'Then take me away with you,' the damsel said. 'If not, I shall kill myself.'

Eliduc again assured her of his deep and unending love. Yet if he were to take her with him, he would be betraying her father, whom he was still under oath to serve. 'But I faithfully promise you,' he said, 'that if you set a day for my return, I shall be there; nothing will prevent me. My life is in your hands.' She named a day on which he was to return for her. They exchanged golden rings, and wept and parted.

Eliduc went to the shore and embarked. The wind was good; the ship sped fast, and he soon reached Brittany. Everyone rejoiced to see him: his lord, his friends, his kin, and most of all his wife. But he himself showed no sense of delight. His manner seemed cold and distant. His thoughts were still on the love that had caught him unawares. His wife felt this especially; had he some heavy secret? Did he believe that she had done wrong while he was out of the country?

'Have you heard false rumours of me, lord?' she said. 'Tell me, for I would defend myself against such lies, even with my life.'

'Lady,' he said, 'I do not accuse you of any crime or misdemeanour while I was absent. With you it could not be! But in the place where I served I vowed to the king that I would return in time of need. That time has now come. As you know, I have to serve my lord here; but when the trouble is cleared I must go without delay. I cannot break my word.' So the lady said no more.

Then Eliduc applied himself to the king's difficulties. On his advice certain steps were taken to guard his land; the invaders were routed and peace at last restored. And now he prepared to leave, for his appointed day of return was drawing near. He took with him only a small trusted company: two nephews, whom he loved; a chamberlain who had been his confidant throughout, and his squire. He wanted no others. All gave an oath of secrecy.

Then, with no more delay he put to sea, and soon reached the English coast.

But he did not want to be seen or recognized, so he took lodgings at some distance from the shore. Then he sent his chamberlain to the damsel, telling her that he had kept his covenant. His chamberlain would bring her to where Eliduc was waiting.

The man disguised himself and went on foot to the city. By devious means he found his way to the damsel's room and told her that the knight had kept his pact. She had been sad and dull, but now she was radiant with pleasure and she kissed the chamberlain many times. He told her to prepare to leave at night-fall, and the rest of the day they spent planning the route, and other details.

When evening fell, the maiden and the young man left the town. She was dressed in a silken garment, finely embroidered with gold, with a short cloak over it. In spite of the sheltering dark, she trembled.

Not far from the city gate, no more than a bow's shot, there was a wood, bordered by fresh green meadowland. There, at the wood's edge, Eliduc waited, and there they met, most joyfully. He set her on his horse, then mounted the steed himself, and they rode to Totnes harbour. A ship lay ready. Only Eliduc and his damsel, and his own men were on board as they set sail.

A good breeze sped them on but, just as they were nearing land, a storm broke, and drove them back to sea. The mast split; the sail was in ribbons. They called upon God, St Nicholas, St Clement and the Virgin Mary to save them. But the ship tossed to and fro, and seemed about to founder.

Then one of the sailors cried out, 'Lord, you have with you the woman who is bringing us all to disaster. We shall never make land while she is here. You have a loyal wife, and now, with this other woman, you are breaking the laws of God. Let us cast her into the sea, and we shall reach harbour safely.'

Eliduc was almost demented with anger. 'Wicked and evil traitor, say no more!' he cried. 'If the lady is harmed, you will pay dearly for it.' He tried to comfort her for she had been suffering from fear and sickness both. But now she received a further pain and shock. The sailor had revealed the fact that Eliduc had a wife in his own country. Deathly pale, she fell face down in a swoon, and did not return to life.

At last Eliduc was convinced that she was dead. He cried out in his anguish, then struck the offending sailor with his oar and pushed him overboard. Then he took the helm himself and steered the vessel to land.

Guilliadun lay as if dead. What was he to do? He would gladly have died with her. He asked his companions for advice, but they had none to give. Certainly the lady must be buried with due honour in consecrated ground, for she was a king's daughter. But where could he find such a place?

An answer came to him. His lodging was near a forest, thirty leagues in circumference, and deep within lived a hermit, a holy man; he had been there forty years and had his own chapel. Eliduc knew this hermit. The chapel would serve well for her burial place. Then he would found an abbey there, and a convent of monks, nuns and canons who would pray for the maiden's soul. He had horses brought; he made his companions swear that they would not betray him, and they rode into the forest. Eliduc carried his beloved before him on his palfrey.

On they rode until they came to the hermit's dwelling. But no one answered them, or opened the chapel door. They looked within. The saintly hermit had passed away, and there was his newly-dug tomb. The men wished to bury the lady straight away, but Eliduc stopped them, saying, 'This would not be correct. I must first consult some wise and holy men about consecrating the place as an abbey or a church. Meanwhile, we shall lay her before the altar and commend her to God.' He had sheets brought, and a kind of bed was made for her. Here she was placed. Eliduc thought that he would die of grief at leaving her there. 'Fair one,' he lamented, 'would that you had never set eyes on me. You would soon have been a queen had you not loved me so purely and faithfully. On the day when you are buried I shall leave the world and take holy orders.' Then he closed the chapel door and departed.

He sent a messenger to tell his wife that he was returning home, and she received him joyfully. But her pleasure was soon chilled, for he spoke little, and no one dared to speak to him. For two days he stayed in the house; then, after early morning mass, he set off for the chapel in the woods. The damsel still lay as if in a swoon, seeming neither to move nor breathe. Yet, strangely, she still had some colour in her cheeks. Eliduc wept, prayed for her soul, and returned, alone, to his home.

His wife began to wonder: where did he go, time after time, when he left the church? She promised one of her servants a large reward if he would follow the knight at a distance and note what direction he took. The man agreed and tracked the knight's path unperceived. He saw Eliduc enter the chapel and come out weeping. The lady was perplexed by this. 'We shall go straightway and visit the hermitage, while my husband is at court speaking with the king. The hermit died not long ago, I believe; my husband knew him, but he surely would not show such violent grief on his account'.

That afternoon, when Eliduc was with the king, the lady went with her page to the hermitage. She entered the chapel and saw at once the maiden on the bed. She was like a new rose. She looked at her lovely face, her slender form, her long arms, her white hands and long fine fingers, and she knew why her husband grieved. She called to her page and showed him the marvel. 'Do you see this damsel, whose beauty is like the rarest gem? This must be my husband's love, for whom he grieves. Indeed, it is no wonder, when so fair a creature is dead.'

She began to weep for the damsel and, as she sat by the bed, a weasel ran past from beneath the altar. The page threw a stick and struck it because it went over the body. He found that he had killed it, and he threw the little corpse on the floor. Soon, another weasel ran out. When it saw the first one lying there, it walked round its head and touched it, piteously, with its paw.

When it did not move, the weasel seemed distressed; it left the chapel and went into the wood in search of herbs. Then, in its teeth, it picked a bright red flower, ran with it into the chapel, and placed it in the mouth of the one that the page had killed. It was restored to life! Seeing this, the lady called out, 'Catch it! Do not let it escape!' The page threw a stick towards the little creature, enough to make it drop the flower. The lady picked up the flower and put it in the mouth of the damsel.

The girl began to breathe; she opened her eyes. 'Have I slept long?' she said.

The lady thanked God, then asked the damsel who she was. 'Lady,' she replied, 'I was born in the land of England, the daughter of a king in that country. I deeply loved a knight, Eliduc, who came to do service for my father. He took me away with him, but he tricked and deceived me, for he has a wife, and this he never revealed. When I learned the truth, I fell into a swoon, and now I find myself here. He has left me lonely and betrayed in a foreign land and I do not know what to do. No maiden should ever trust a man.'

'Fair damsel,' the lady said, 'the knight Eliduc feels no joy, for he thinks that you are dead. He comes here every day to look at you, and he weeps. I must tell you that I am his wife, and my heart grieves for him in his sorrow. I wished to know what caused it, and where he went alone. So I followed the path and found you; what is more, I discovered a way to bring you back to life. I am overjoyed that you are alive. You must come with me and return to the one who so dearly loves you. I shall set him free completely, and take the veil.' The maiden was comforted, and together they went back to the lady's home.

The lady now called a trusted servant and sent him to find her husband and tell him that the damsel had been restored to life, and was now in his own home. Eliduc listened with wonder, mounted his horse and rode back to the castle. His beloved was alive! Never had he felt so joyful. But first he thanked his wife most courteously for her goodness and for finding the means of working this miracle. The lady looked at her husband and at the damsel and saw their happiness. Then she said that she would withdraw from the marriage; she wished to become a nun and serve God. If Eliduc would give her some land, she would found an abbey; then he might marry the damsel. To have two wives was neither right nor proper, nor did the law permit it.

Eliduc willingly gave her lands and funds, and the lady had a church built near the hermitage chapel in the wood. When all was complete she took the veil and thirty nuns came with her. There she established her order.

Eliduc married his damsel; they lived together for many a year, with perfect love between them. But a time came when they chose to turn to God. Near to his castle Eliduc built a church and monastery which he endowed with most of his land and all his gold and silver. Here he placed men of his own household and other pious persons to maintain the holy place. When all the work was done, he himself entered the order. His wife went to the house of the Abbess, who had been the first wife of Eliduc. The Abbess received her with honour and welcome, as if she were her own sister, and herself instructed her in the convent's rules. They prayed for Eliduc, whom both had loved, and Eliduc prayed for them, sending messengers often to see how they fared and if they were content. All three in time came to a good and godly end.

From the tale of these three, the courtly Bretons in bygone times composed a lay, that they should not be forgotten.

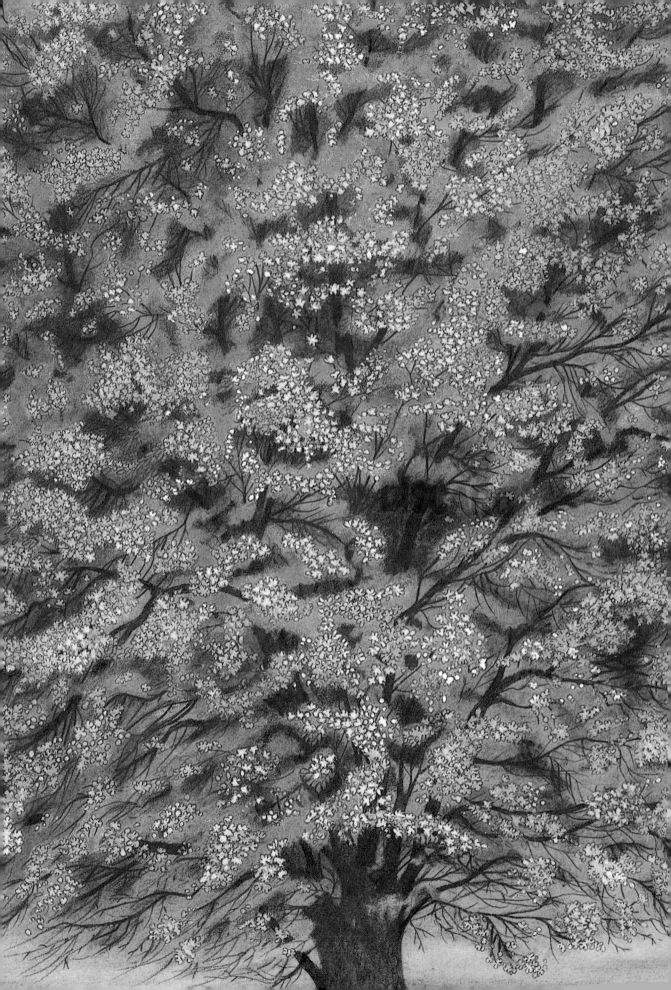